REQUIEM FOR A DREAM

REQUIEM FOR A DREAM

Screenplay by
Darren Aronofsky
and
Hubert Selby, Jr

faber and faber

First published in 2000
by Faber and Faber Limited
3 Queen Square London WC1N 3AU

Published in the United States by Faber and Faber, Inc.,
an affiliate of Farrar, Straus and Giroux LLC, New York

Photoset by Parker Typesetting Service, Leicester
Printed in England by Mackays of Chatham PLC, Chatham, Kent

A CIP record for this book
is available from the British Library

ISBN 0-571-20631-x

2 4 6 8 10 9 7 5 3 1

CONTENTS

INTRODUCTION

Cannes Film Festival, 18 May 2000

MILES FIELDER: *You've never made any secret of the fact that you're a great admirer of Hubert Selby Jr's work. How did you come to work with the man himself?*

DARREN ARONOFSKY: The first time I met Hubert was when I was at film school in the early nineties, and I did a short film [*Fortune Cookie*] based on one of his stories. I actually called up the Writers' Guild to see if I could just connect with him, and they gave me his home phone number instead of his agent's. That's how accessible he is – he's listed in the phone book. So I called him up, and he invited me over. I was expecting this mean guy with a sledgehammer, and he turned out to be really sweet. I only hung out with him for ten or fifteen minutes, and it was so weird: because I was thinking, 'This is Selby, the man about violence, and pain . . .' And back then I completely missed what he was really about.

Have you figured it out since then?
I've always been in awe of his writing, but I never really quite got him as a person. It took me all this time, probably right up until this week, to work through it and get to a place where I'm in complete awe of him. For one thing, he's much older than me. But it's also because of the state he's in – which is that he's a completely enlightened human being. I say that honestly. I know it can be laughed at – whatever . . . He's been dropping the science: he's a teacher, a sensi, a master of life. He's filled with love, filled with creative energy. And what comes out of his mouth is completely inspirational. I think Ellen Burstyn was in awe of him too, and for me Ellen is one of the greatest people on this planet – definitely one of the greatest artists I've ever been next to. There's a term in Buddhism – I can't remember it exactly, but it means 'someone who returns to help people', and that's what Ellen called Hubert. And really, that's what his deal is. For some reason, he writes about the depths of humanity, he shows how human we are by showing how much we can collapse. And by doing that, he's

actually showing a light. Some of the best compliments I've had for *Requiem* have come from people telling me how elated they were coming out of it, or how elated they felt two days after seeing it.

So at what point did you decide to turn Selby's novel into a film?
During the editing of π we acquired the rights to the book for like $1000, which was a lot of fucking money back then. And it was really hard to get, because we were broke working on π. But we believed in the material so tremendously, we were so passionate. We thought, 'Everyone's going to say "No" to this' – and, in fact everyone did say 'No', and everyone continues to say 'No'. But as my producer Eric Watson says, 'When everyone tells you you're doing something wrong, you know you're doing something right.' I really believe that. However people respond to the movie, the *depth* of how they respond to it answers all my questions about whether it works or not.

How did you and Selby collaborate on the script?
Hubert lives in L.A. and I live in New York, so it was a long-distance collaboration. He had written a script of *Requiem for a Dream* about twenty years ago for a different producer, but he'd lost it. So I sat down to write it, and about three-quarters of the way through he called me up and said, 'I was in my mom's home and I found a copy of that old script.' He sent it over, and it was amazing – because almost every single scene he had chosen to put in the film, I had chosen too. The connection was really there, as far as the essence of the novel was concerned. So I incorporated his ideas and continued on my draft, then I sent it to him and we went back and forth on drafts, we'd give each other notes. Sometimes when you condense a novel into a screenplay, certain holes appear, because you shrink things and you put different scenes next to each other, and you find that you're missing something. So you have to create a little bridge. Sometimes I'd ask him to write a little dialog, and he'd scribble it out on a napkin and send it my way.

Ellen Burstyn is enjoying something of a revival at the moment. Hers is such a brave performance – there's absolutely no vanity there.
And I had the camera about a millimeter from her face . . . This is a great actor. She's always working towards bettering her art. When I

wrapped with Ellen, I was like, 'Few people get to play with Michael Jordan every day.' I felt like a high school coach working with one of the greatest basketball players in the world. She really could do anything. And every day she'd come to set and just blow our minds. I had big, hairy union grips sitting around scene after scene, just sobbing – or walking off set because they couldn't handle it. The sad thing is that she's now going to go back and play grandmother roles and mother roles – and by that, I mean 'normal' mother roles, as opposed to this one. But it's just really hard for these great artists to get the challenging roles they deserve.

The film's setting, Coney Island, feels like it's another character in the film.
The novel is set in the Bronx, but I moved it to Coney Island, Brooklyn. Partly it's because that's where I come from, I grew up right outside Coney Island, in a neighborhood called Manhattan Beach, which is talked about in the film. Coney Island has always been an aesthetic inspiration for me, because a dying amusement park has so much nostalgia. But there's another reason for setting the film there, and it's because I was trying to make a fable. The characters speak this weird language, they wear different types of clothes. There's modern technology; you're not really sure what timeframe it is. I felt that the nostalgic atmosphere of Coney Island would help that, because it makes the world of the film much more like a dreamland. In fact, one of the big parks on Coney Island at the turn of the century was called Dream Land. It burned down around 1904 . . .

The film's music is obviously motivated by something much deeper than just the action. Were you trying to create a specific emotional impact there?
There are a lot of different combinations of music in the film; they all come from one creator, Clint Mansell, who, as you may know, was the front-man for Pop Will Eat Itself, and also composed π. There's the overture, a repeating piece of music that combines the flowing classical strings of the Kronos Quartet with electronic samples. And for Clint to go from 'Big Mac & Fries' to working with the Kronos Quartet is quite a career! The rhythm was his own sample, made out of punches from a Bruce Lee movie. Combined with the strings, they create that beautiful overture. And then there's the music from the third act, the winter: that

jarring, intense sound, which we call 'Mansell's Requiem'. That was created in an amazing way. We went around listening to our favorite parts of all the great requiems, from Mozart to Verdi. Then we basically chose interesting notes, and Clint sampled them into a drum machine and played it percussively. And then we brought that to the Kronos Quartet, and they played over it. So it was a real experiment. I think Clint has an unbelievable natural ability, to understand stories and narratives and turn them into musical ideas. That's what the greatest composers do.

You've referred to certain passages in the film as 'hip-hop montages'. Can you explain what they are?
We call them hip-hop montages, but I've gotta come up with a better term than that, it doesn't sound so cool. Basically it comes out of the fact that I grew up back in the 80s in Brooklyn, very much into hip-hop culture. All the music we listened to was rap; all the dancing we did was break. There were some films on hip-hop back then, but it's always been a big part of me, and I've always wanted to figure out some ways to use hip-hop techniques in film, as a very, very quick way to deliver information to the audience. I think I first started it in that first short film of Selby's, back in 1992, 1993. And I developed it in π: those sequences where it's 'Flip lid, pill, gulp, swallow. Flip lid, pill, gulp, swallow.' The point of the montages in *Requiem* is to demonstrate the repetitive, obsessive nature of addiction, as well as to draw a connection between all the different addictions in the film: TV, coffee, drugs – they're all the same. It doesn't matter what the chemical is, the result affects your body, and it helps you to believe in the dream. The montages were always a very calculated element, and hopefully they really build out of the story. The biggest insult you can give me is, 'It's like MTV.' That's just a joke. First of all, we cut a lot quicker than MTV: each of those shots is one-third of a second. MTV is style over substance; or style *without* substance, I should say. It's basically just cool shots. With *Requiem* we tried to discipline ourselves as much as possible, to make sure that every single stylistic element that we chose in the film had a narrative reason. If it didn't have a narrative reason, it couldn't be in the movie. Period. So the montages became a narrative element, a film-grammatical element to help tell the story. It had to be like a

word that got repeated over and over again; so that every stylistic choice gets repeated and, hopefully, it has a pay-off. With the hip-hop montages the goal for the dramatic pay-off was the big dramatic moment when he sticks the needle in the hole. The hip-hop montage breaks in the middle, before the eyeball pay-off at the end. It breaks, pauses for a second: he puts the needle in his arm. And then it cuts back to the montage. Most people don't see that, because they're not looking at the screen at that point. But I tried to make a statement there about how the characters are making a major choice about following their dream, and thereby abandoning their humanity and the chance that they could save themselves.

What about the use of split-screen?
π was a purely subjective movie; the goal was to tell a story purely from the POV of Max's brain. Part of the reason I was attracted to *Requiem* was that it was extremely subjective material, except the added complexity of having four characters really intrigued me. Then I realized that in my opening scene I had my two main characters interacting – how do I show their different subjectivities? I thought of the idea of using split-screen, of really demonstrating that we had two films here, and that we have two main stories going on, and also that the two characters are apart, they're not connected.

That works very effectively during the love scene in which two people share the same bed, but their pillow talk is split into two images.
I have a really hard time doing love scenes. I mean how many love scenes have you seen that are really cool or different? So rarely do you see a sex scene where there's more to it than just a little titillation. So for me to do a sex scene, I wanted to make it interesting. So I did the split-screen and then I did the spiralling shot later. But the split-screen is one area where the film does have problems, because it doesn't pay off – it seems like it's just sort of gimmick. I'd say it *does* pay off on DVD, which has some missing scenes. I went for a triple split-screen later in the film; I was going for a real climactic moment there, but it slowed down the film so we took it out. We had this amazing shot where they're all flipping out: three rows of their eyes, bugging out, vibrating. It was awesome, really cool. But sometimes you gotta cut out cool stuff.

Is it a concern of yours to be seen to be preaching about drug abuse?
We all know that drugs are dangerous. That's one reading of the film, but it's a top-level reading. The next level is about the struggle of addiction versus the human spirit. The struggle of wanting to lose weight is the same struggle as wanting to quit cigarettes. It's an addiction to a dream of yourself: wanting to be skinny, or healthy. And it's an addiction that's extremely dangerous, because we can believe in the dream to such an extent that we don't live the present, we don't change our lives now, and that can lead to a collapse, like in the book. Then there's another message about the myth of the American Dream, which is what makes Selby such an archetypal American writer – because all of his material is about that myth. Selby says that the educational system in America tells us that we are all born jerk-offs, and that the goal is to make us rich jerk-offs. Selby talks about 'unlearning the lies'. There are all these lies we're given, which are basically an opiate; the opiate of the masses, the American Dream. Then there's another message about living in the present as opposed to living in the future. So, yes drugs are bad, and if people walk away with that, fine. But hopefully there's a deeper emotional thing going on. I have tried to live a life where I experience everything. I've never been addicted to drugs, but I understand that addiction. Sometimes drugs make you feel really good, and sometimes you play around a little too much. I've never gone too far myself, but I've had many friends who have. And I think drug addiction is totally understandable to all of us. Supposedly, quitting nicotine is harder than quitting dope. And I'll tell you, trying to lose forty or fifty pounds is pretty fucking hard . . .

What do you feel about the way the film has unsettled some audience members? Is using terrible images necessary to get your message across these days?
Definitely, in these days, I think audiences are extremely over-saturated with a tremendous amount of imagery. There are a lot of people who won't be able to handle the film, and there are a lot of people for whom it will be light in some way. People see a lot of sick shit today, especially on the Internet. The most disturbing images get circulated. I can only imagine what kind of stuff I would be exposed to now, if I were thirteen again. I guarantee

you, in four or five years, any image in this film is going to look light. I hope the emotional impact will still be there, but in terms of the shock value, it's really not that cutting edge. The bottom line is this: perhaps the most disturbing shot is the needle in the hole, in the open wound. There was a lot of debate about that between the studio and me, as you can imagine. For me, that image, that one shot completely sums up what the movie is about; which is how far we will go to deny our existence in the present, and live in the fantasy of a dream. How far we will go to hold onto that dream, to fill that hole inside of us, with any addiction, rather than face the reality that is happening now. There's no possible way I would ever remove that shot, because as soon as you start pulling those punches, then why the hell are you making this movie? This movie is totally about going as far as the collapse can go, the lowest depths humanity can take us to. It's *Requiem for a Dream*, it's a song for the death of a dream. And what this song is about is how deep that death is. That's why it gets so extreme.

Requiem for a Dream

ON THE TV –

– is Tappy Tibbons, America's favorite television personality. His charismatic personality shines for the entire world to see.

His audience cheers wildly.

AUDIENCE
Juice by Tappy! Juice by Tappy! Juice by Tappy! ooooOOOOH! Tappy's got juice! Tappy's got juice! ooooOOOOH Tappy!

TAPPY TIBBONS
Thank you! Thank you! Thank you very much! Today's winner is a flight attendant from Washington DC. Will you please welcome Mary –

Suddenly, the plug is pulled. The TV flickers off and we –

CUT TO:

THE PRESENTATION TITLES, THEN –

CUT TO:

INT. SARA'S LIVING ROOM – DAY

Harry Goldfarb, young twenties, is an eccentric kid with a seductive smile.

He tries to stop his mother, Sara Goldfarb, from locking herself in the closet.

HARRY
Ma! Ma! C'mon, Ma!

SARA
Harold. Please. Not again the TV.

She slams the door closed and Harry talks to the shut door.

HARRY

Why do you haveta make such a big deal out of this? Eh? You know you'll have the set back in a couple of hours.

No answer.

Why ya gotta make me feel guilty?
(*frustrated*)
Ahhh . . .

Harry walks across the room to the early eighties TV with ridiculous rabbit ears.

Sara locks the door and retreats to the back of the closet.

Harry starts to push the set on its stand when suddenly it jerks – almost falling. Harry spies a thick bicycle chain going from around the TV to the radiator.

Jesus! Whatta ya tryin' to do, eh? You tryin' to get me to break my own mother's set? Or break the radiator?

Harry marches to the closet.

. . . an' maybe blow up the whole house? You tryin' to make me a killer? Your own son? Your own flesh and blood? WHATTA YA DOIN' TA ME? YOUR OWN SON!!!

Then, a thin key slowly peeks out from under the closet door. Harry works it out with his fingernail and yanks it up.

Why do you always gotta play games with my head for krist's sake? Don't you have any considerations for my feelings? Why do you haveta make my life so difficult?

And then, meekly from the closet –

SARA

Harold, I wouldn't. The chain isn't for you. The robbers.

HARRY

Then why didn't you tell me? The set almost fell. I coulda had a heart attack.

Sara shakes her head in the darkness.

4

SARA

You should be well, Harold.

HARRY

Then why won't you come out?

Harry tries to open the locked closet door but can't.

See what I mean? See how you always gotta upset me?

Harry walks to the TV, unlocks the chain and starts to wheel the TV towards the front door. He pauses by the closet.

Ma? Ma? C'mon out? Please, Ma.

No response. Inside, Sara hugs her knees.

Then, he throws up his hands, mumbles –

Eh, screw it.

– and pushes the set carefully out of the apartment.

In the closet, Sara hears the door shut. She mumbles to herself –

SARA

It's not happening. And if it should be happening it would be alright, so don't worry, Seymour. It'll all work out. You'll see already. In the end it's all nice.

SMASH CUT TO:

BLACK –

– AND THE TITLE: 'REQUIEM FOR A DREAM'

TITLES BEGIN –

EXT. SARA'S APARTMENT – HALLWAY – CONTINUOUS

Waiting for Harry is Tyrone C. Love, young twenties, leaning against the wall, playing skillfully with a yo-yo.

Taking his time, Tyrone helps Harry wheel the set to the dingy elevator.

TYRONE

Sheeit, this mutha startin' to look a little seedy, man.

HARRY
What's the matta, ya particular all of a sudden?

TYRONE
Hey, baby, ah don't care if it's growin' hair just so's we get our braid.

CUT TO:

EXT. SARA'S BUILDING – BRIGHTON BEACH, BROOKLYN – DAY

Lining the front of the building in beach chairs are ten female Yentas absorbing the sun and passing judgement on Harry.

Harry says hello and is greeted by a chorus of fake, sarcastic 'hellos' in return.

CUT TO:

EXT. STREETS OF BRIGHTON BEACH AND CONEY ISLAND

Harry and Tyrone carefully navigate the TV through the streets of the old Brooklyn neighborhood.

They go under the elevated train, past the giant, dying projects, across the boardwalk, beneath the shadows of the towering parachute jump and through the cracking and boarded-up amusement park.

THE TITLES END.

A HARD CUT TO:

BLACK

ON THE SCREEN IN WHITE LETTERS: 'SUMMER'

CUT TO:

INT. PAWN SHOP – DAY

Old and squat Mr Rabinowitz shakes his head as Harry and Tyrone push the set into his store.

He stands behind a cage of bulletproof glass with all of the pawn shop's possessions.

> MR RABINOWITZ
> So look, the table too already.

> HARRY
> Hey, what do you want from me? I can't schlep it on my back.

> MR RABINOWITZ
> You got a friend.

> TYRONE
> Hey man, I ain't my leper's schlepper.

Harry chuckles.

> MR RABINOWITZ
> Such a son. A goniff. Your mother needs you like a moose needs a hat rack.

The pawn shop owner clucks his tongue and slowly counts out the money.

CUT TO:

QUICK HIP-HOP MONTAGE:

Lighter flicks–liquid on spoon sizzles–tourniquet snaps–needle sucks–hand slaps vein–a thunderous rush of liquid–and finally an ecstatic sigh.

INT. TYRONE'S DIVE PAD – LATER

Tyrone's pad is run down but it'll do. Tight on Harry back-spinning a record on the turntable and halting the beat. Then he lets the other turntable spin and start a new tune.

> TYRONE
>
> Sheeit, that's some boss scag, baby. I mean DYN-A-MITE.

> HARRY
>
> Yeah, man, something else.

Harry calmly watches the record spin.

CUT TO:

INT. DONUT SHOP – NIGHT – LATER

Tyrone and Harry sit at the counter of an all-night donut shop, sipping hot chocolate and eating chocolate Crullers.

> TYRONE
>
> Ya know what we oughta do, man? Huh? We oughta get a piece of this Brody shit and cut it and off it, ya dig?

> HARRY
>
> This stuff's good enough to cut in half and still get you wasted. We could double our money. Easy.

> TYRONE
>
> That's right. An' then we buy a couple a pieces an' we got something' else goin', man. It sure would be righteous.

> HARRY
>
> In no time we'd get a pound of pure straight from Sal the Geep.

> TYRONE
>
> No hassles. That's all I want, no hassles.

Just then, a hulking Cop sits down on the stool next to Harry.

Tyrone and Harry both fall silent and slowly sip their hot chocolates.

Harry looks down at the Cop's gun. It's maybe six inches from his hand.

Slowly, he reaches over and undoes the safety latch on the Cop's holster.

Tyrone's eyes fill with fear.

The Waitress comes over and gives the Cop his coffee.

WAITRESS

Can I get you a –

Just then, Harry yanks the gun out of the holster. The Cop spins around. Harry retreats –

COP

Hey! Hey!

Harry smiles as the Cop charges. Tyrone snickers. Then Harry tosses the gun over the Cop's head. Tyrone catches it. The Cop chases Tyrone.

Harry and Tyrone laugh as they toss the gun back and forth just over the frustrated Cop's head. The Cop slips and falls on his ass and we –

CUT BACK TO:

Reality. Five minutes earlier –

WAITRESS

Anything else? Huh?

Tyrone butts Harry. Harry looks up at the Waitress who stares at him. The towering Cop looks over as well.

Well.

HARRY

No, no. Just the check.

The Cop returns to his donut.

CUT TO:

INT. PAWN SHOP – DAY

Mr Rabinowitz shakes his head as Sara enters. He pulls out a ledger book that is labeled 'Sara Goldfarb's TV'.

9

MR RABINOWITZ

Good evening, Mrs Goldfarb.

SARA

Good evening, Mr Rabinowitz, though I'm not so sure how good it is. And you?

MR RABINOWITZ

Uh, so what can I say? Are you wanting your TV?

SARA

Yes, if you don't mind.

Sara pulls a crinkled ten dollar bill out of the corner of her blouse and hands it to Mr Rabinowitz.

MR RABINOWITZ

Mrs Goldfarb, can I ask you a question, you won't be taking it personal?

Sara shrugs.

How many years we know each other?
            (*he nods his head*)
Who's to count? Why don't you tell already the police so maybe they could talk to Harry and he wouldn't be stealing no more the TV.

SARA

Oooo, Mr Rabinowitz, I couldn't, Harold's my only child. He's all I have.

CUT TO:

INT. SARA'S LIVING ROOM – LATER

Sara chains the TV to the radiator again. She turns on the set, adjusts the rabbit ears and watches whatever is on.

Sara smiles as she settles into her chair. She ceremoniously removes the plastic wrapper from around a box of chocolates.

Immediately, she pulls out a chocolate, covered cream and lets it dissolve in her mouth. Her eyes shut in gentle ecstasy.

CUT TO:

EXT. SEACOAST TOWER – DAY

Looking straight up at the thirty-storey building with sharp eyes is Marion. She is beautiful, fresh, and in her young twenties.

Harry, with a stack of newspapers under his arm, comes up from behind and kisses her on the neck.

CUT TO:

SEACOAST TOWER'S FOYER

Harry randomly presses one of countless buzzers. An Old Lady responds a moment later:

OLD LADY

Hello? Who is it?

Harry mumbles into the speaker. He and Marion try to hold their laughter.

Who?

Harry mumbles again. When the buzzer rings we're on –

THE ELEVATOR

– in black-and-white video. A security camera watches Harry and Marion jump around as they head to the –

TOP FLOOR

PING! Harry dips his head out the open doors.

All clear. He grabs Marion and they dash to the –

STAIRWELL

– where red, bold warnings on the emergency exit roof door threaten alarm if the door is opened.

MARION

What do we do now?

Harry pulls out a wire from his back pocket and shorts the alarm.

Then, he kicks the roof door open. White light rushes in.

CUT TO:

INT. SARA'S LIVING ROOM

Her phone rrrings and Sara leans towards it but she continues to adjust the rabbit ears on her set, torn between the priority of the two activities.

Finally, four rings later, she lunges for the phone and flops down in her viewing chair. She is greeted by a Cheery Voice.

> SARA

Hello?

> CHEERY VOICE
> (*off-screen*)

Mrs Goldfarb? Mrs Sara Goldfarb?

> SARA

It's me. Speaking.

The voice is so enthusiastic that she looks over to the TV to see if it's coming from there.

> CHEERY VOICE
> (*off-screen*)

Mrs Goldfarb, this is Lyle Russel from Malin & Block.

> SARA

I'm not interested in –

> CHEERY VOICE
> (*off-screen*)

Wait, Mrs Goldfarb. I'm not selling anything. Nothing. I just want to offer you a chance to be on television.

> SARA

Television?

> CHEERY VOICE
> (*off-screen*)

That's right, Mrs Goldfarb.

SARA

Look, I don't have any –

CHEERY VOICE
(*off-screen*)
I'm not looking for money, Mrs Goldfarb. I'm calling to tell
you you've already won. Your name was selected from a long
list of available contestants. You've been chosen and you now
have an opportunity to be on television.

SARA

Me? On television?

Sara's eyes light up.

LYLE RUSSEL
(*off-screen*)
That's right, Mrs Goldfarb. You on television.

SARA

I never thought I'd be on television. I'm just a –

LYLE RUSSEL
(*off-screen*)
Malin & Block discovers contestants for most of America's
favorite television shows.

SARA

Ooooooo . . . Me . . . me . . . on . . . oh I can't . . .

LYLE RUSSEL
(*off-screen*)
Yes, Mrs Goldfarb, *you*. Congratulations! I can't tell you why
you are so lucky, but you are. Congratulations!

*Sara falls against the back of the viewing chair, one hand clutches
desperately at the phone, the other on top of her dress. Her eyes bulge,
her mouth hangs open.*

You will receive all necessary information in the mail, Mrs
Goldfarb. Goodbye and . . . God bless.

*Click! Sara tries to catch her breath. She awakens from her ecstasy
when the phone beeps its off-the-hook sound.*

CUT TO:

INT. SARA'S BEDROOM – A BIT LATER

Sara picks up a framed photo. The picture was taken on Harry's high school graduation day years ago. Harry, in the middle, is an eighteen-year-old in cap and gown. Sara's husband Seymour hovers over Harry's left shoulder.

On Harry's right is a younger-looking Sara. She is thirty pounds lighter, has brilliant red hair and wears a red dress and gold shoes. Sara stares at her outfit.

Then she rushes to the closet. As she hums a tuneless monotone, she carefully pulls out the last dress on the hook. She ceremoniously removes the dry-cleaning plastic and smiles at her red dress.

She puts it on. In the mirror she looks over one shoulder and then the other. She tries to zip up the back, but after half an inch and many minutes of exertion she gives up.

On her hands and knees, she searches through mounds of shoes for the special pair. She pulls out the gold shoes and dusts them off. Shakily, Sara puts them on. She smiles at herself in the mirror.

CUT TO:

EXT. ROOF – DAY

Harry and Marion throw paper airplanes down on the dying amusement park.

> HARRY
> . . . but why you so hard on your folks? I mean, they give you the bread for rent, money for the shrink –

> MARION
> They bug me. They're fucking hypocrites.

Harry shrugs – no big deal.

> MARION
> Like they're in that big house with all their cars and money. They pay me off so they don't have to deal with me. They pay

off charities to deal with their racism. Then we'll see how liberal they are when I come home with a black guy.

                              HARRY

You know what you gotta do.

                              MARION

Yeah.

                              HARRY

You gotta get away from them.

                              MARION

How?

                              HARRY

What about your clothes? Maybe you could sell them. Open a store.

                              MARION

I can't.

                              HARRY

Why?

                              MARION

When will I have time to hang with you?

A deserved kiss.

CUT TO:

EXT. ADA'S APARTMENT — HALLWAY — CONTINUOUS

Sara, barely wearing her red dress, knocks on a door. Ada, an orange-haired woman Sara's age, answers the door.

                              ADA

So where's the party?

                              SARA

Party, schmarty. This is like all the parties. When I tell you, you'll jump out the window.

                              ADA

A basement window, I hope.

CUT TO:

INT. SARA'S BEDROOM

Ada tries to stuff Sara into her red dress but it ain't happening.

> ADA
> Well, I have a great diet book.

> SARA
> *Zophtic.*

CUT BACK TO:

EXT. EMERGENCY EXIT DOOR

Marion grabs Harry's short-circuit wire. Harry, who's already inside, looks at his girl's mischievous eyes.

> HARRY
> Marion!

Harry gets it. He smiles. Then, Marion yanks the wire.

ALARMS SCREAM!!!

Harry and Marion bolt to the –

TOP FLOOR

– where both elevators charge the top floor.

> MARION
> They're coming.

Harry grabs Marion's hand and pulls her down the hallway.

Dead end.

Harry and Marion squeeze against the doorway – fighting the urge to crack-up. Then:

PING! – the elevator. A Security Guard charges out.

Marry and Marion hold their breath. The Guard heads straight for the staircase.

Then our criminals charge –

THE ELEVATOR

– and in black-and-white video make out all the way down.

THEN:

EXT. SEACOAST TOWER – DAY

Harry and Marion burst out of the front door laughing, alarms ringing behind them.

CUT TO:

INT. SARA'S MAILBOX – DAY

The mailbox opens and Sara disappointedly peers into the empty darkness.

CUT TO:

INT. SARA'S APARTMENT

Sara sits in her viewing chair watching television and reading her diet book as she slides herself a chocolate. The diet book is called 'Ten Pounds in Ten Days.'

She flips through about a hundred pages of introduction until she comes to the words, 'FIRST WEEK.'

She stares at the page and suddenly she becomes concerned. She reaches for a chocolate-covered caramel as we read the page with her:

BREAKFAST

1 hard-boiled egg
$\frac{1}{2}$ grapefruit
1 cup black coffee (*no* sugar)

LUNCH

1 hard-boiled egg
$\frac{1}{2}$ grapefruit
$\frac{1}{2}$ cup lettuce (*no* dressing)
1 cup black coffee (*no* sugar)

1 hard-boiled egg
½ grapefruit
1 cup black coffee (*no* sugar)
NOTE: Drink at least 2 quarts of water each day.

Sara stares and chews.

*Her eyes focus on the words, 'no' '1,' and '½'. They focus on the
repetition of meals. They focus on the insanity, searching for the real
information between the lines.*

*She hears a giggle and turns to look at the refrigerator. The fridge
tremors slightly – a small mechanical rattle.*

*Defeated, she drops the book and reaches for another chocolate. Her
head starts to hang and tears begin to well up in her eyes.*

But then she notices something on the television.

TAPPY TIBBONS

Now, let's meet our next winner. Straight from Brighton
Beach, Brooklyn, let's give a juicy welcome to Mrs Sara
Goldfarb.

*There she is! Herself dressed in red, her hair gorgeous red, walking across
the screen, so slim, so trim, so sexy. Such curves. This is Red Sara.*

Our Sara's tears fade as her chin lifts and she begins to smile.

*She watches Red Sara pose for the television audience. She can hear the
applause and the wolf whistles.*

She puts the chocolates away and lifts up the book – new hope.

CUT TO:

INT. MARION'S APARTMENT – MIDSUMMER DAY

*Bright, summer sun shoots through the window and screams across
Marion's living room floor until it slows and falls upon Harry and
Marion.*

They are asleep, fully dressed in each other's arms.

The racing sounds of the outside midday summer traffic dissipate and they are alone in a vacuum of melodious heartbeats and deep breaths.

CUT TO:

INT. SARA'S APARTMENT – DAY

Ada strips Sara's hair with a smelly home-made peroxide concoction at the sink. They're positioned so that they can both watch the TV set from the corners of their eyes.

> SARA
>
> Ech, what a smell. That's the Gawanus Canal?

> ADA
>
> Just relax, Dolly, you got a long way to go. You'll get used to it.

> SARA
>
> Get used to it? I'm almost losing my appetite.

They chuckle.

> When's lunch?

Bigger laugh.

> ADA
>
> Sweetie, we're lucky if we're finished before supper.

> SARA
>
> So long?

> ADA
>
> That's right. With you we're starting from scratch one.

> SARA
>
> And I thought I would catch a little sun today.

> ADA
>
> In a box you'll catch it. You just relax and think how gorgeous you'll look with your red hair. Today the hair, tomorrow the sun.

CUT TO:

INT. MARION'S KITCHEN

Marion straightens up the kitchen. Harry is spinning some records on his portable turntable. Tyrone plays with his yo-yo.

MARION
Anybody wanna waste some time?

Marion pulls out three pills. Harry and Tyrone each grab one. Ingestion . . .

WIDE SHOT *of the kitchen in time lapse. The next three-minute scene is actually a three-hour event as Harry, Marion and Tyrone hang out. We listen to them at normal, if not slightly slowed down, speed.*

HARRY
I'm starving.

TYRONE
Yeah, me too, get me a Snickers.

HARRY
Damn, Ty, don't you eat anything except Snickers?

TYRONE

Yeah, Chuckles. Ah digs Chuckles.

MARION

You sure as hell don't know anything about eating, man.

HARRY

What you need is some good noodle soup.

TYRONE

Sheeit, Pepsi and Snickers'll take care of anything.

HARRY

And maybe some bread.

TYRONE

I prefer the type that goes in my pocket not my mouth.

HARRY

Exactly. Angel told me about a job –

In the flash of an eye, Harry changes record after record, Tyrone rolls a joint and Marion lights some candles.

TYRONE

A job! Hah!

MARION

What? You lose a bet?

TYRONE
(*giggles*)
Damn, this is a righteous chick, Jim.

HARRY

No, we got this idea. Tyrone has this connection, Brody, with some dynamite shit. If we can get some cash together we can get a piece, cut it up and make a fortune.

TYRONE

Soon we could get a pound of pure and retire.

HARRY

We'd get off hard knocks and be on easy street.

Someone is at the door. Marion answers it and seven friends pile in.

Everyone is in time lapse and everyone is partying. We watch and listen to the evening's festivities until –

MARION

What's the catch?

Suddenly, the racing kitchen clock stops.

CUT TO:

INT. SARA'S BATHROOM – DAY

Sara stares in the mirror, blinking at her ridiculously orange hair. It's nowhere near red.

SARA

That's red?

ADA

Well, it's not exactly red but it's almost, maybe, in the same family.

SARA

The same family? They're not even distant cousins already.

ADA

It's a red. Not a red red, but a red.

SARA

Red? You're telling me this is a red?

ADA

Yeah. I'm telling. It's a red.

SARA

Then what's orange? If this is a red I want to know what's orange?

Ada looks at Sara's hair, then her reflection, then back to Sara's hair and then back to her reflection. She purses her lips and shrugs.

ADA

Well, it could be a little orange, too.

SARA

A little orange? It's a little orange like being a little pregnant.

ADA
(*shrugs*)
So what's to worry? It'll be alright.

SARA
What's to worry? Someone may try to juice me.

ADA
Relax, relax, Dolly. It just needs a little more dye. It'll be alright for television.

SARA
All day long, I'm getting my scalp scraped and burned and smelling like dead fish and I look like a basketball.

ADA
Relax. You should learn to relax. That's your trouble, you don't know how to relax already. I'm telling you it's alright. Tomorrow we'll do it again and you'll look like Lucille Ball.

Ada leads Sara away from the mirror.

CUT TO:

INT. MARION'S APARTMENT – DAY

(*Post-sex*) + (*pre-sleep*) = (*intimate talk*)

HARRY
You know something? I've always thought you are the most beautiful woman I've ever seen.

MARION
Really?

HARRY
Since the first time I met you.

MARION
That's nice, Harry. That really makes me feel good.

HARRY
Good for your ego, eh?

MARION

Well, I can't say that it does it any harm, but that's not what I
mean. It makes me feel good all over, like . . . well, you know
lots of people tell me that and it's meaningless, completely
meaningless.

HARRY

You mean because you think they're putting you on?

MARION

No, no, nothing like that. I don't know or care if they are. I
guess maybe they really mean it, but from them it just doesn't
mean anything to me. When you say it, I hear it. You know
what I mean? I really hear it.

HARRY

Someone like you could really make it alright for me.

MARION

You think?

HARRY

Yeah. I've been thinking . . .

Harry drifts off. Marion's interest is sparked.

MARION

What?

*Harry looks at Marion. A beat. Then he gets the courage. He jumps out
of bed.*

HARRY

Here.

He pulls Marion. She laughs:

MARION

What?

CUT TO:

INT. MARION'S KITCHEN

*Harry in a shirt stands over Marion who's wrapped in a sheet. They
lean over a folder on the kitchen table.*

24

MARION

What is it?

HARRY

You remember when I told you about the store. Well, I've
been thinking about it. I put together some numbers and it's
not impossible. I think you can do it. We should do it. We
can do it together.

MARION

How long have you been thinking about this?

HARRY

Not so long. Since we started hanging out.

A pause. Marion thinks.

MARION

It's a great idea.

HARRY

Yeah?

MARION

It is. Let's do it. Let's open it in the city. How do we start?

HARRY

Well, first me and Ty gotta get money for the piece and
then –

MARION

I'll get it.

HARRY

Nah.

MARION

No, I can.

HARRY

Really? How?

MARION

How do you think? My fucking parents.

A laugh. And then they hug and kiss gently.

Harry pulls his face back a few inches from Marion's.

HARRY

I think I'm falling in love with you.

MARION

Think?

TIGHT SHOTS *and* QUICK CUTS *as Harry kisses the tip of Marion's nose, then her eyelids, then her cheeks and her soft lips, her chin, her neck and lastly her ear lobes.*

Then he whispers in her ear:

HARRY

Marion, Marion, I love you.

FADE TO BLINDING WHITE — THEN:

INT. SARA'S MAILBOX — DAY

We pull out of the white and into Sara's mailbox. She peeks in — empty.

CUT TO:

INT. SARA'S KITCHEN — DAY

TIGHT ON *kitchen clock ticking normally.*

ON *Sara's breakfast — one hard-boiled egg, half a grapefruit and a mug of black coffee.*

ON *the directions in Sara's diet book.*

ON *Sara — blinking at her 'meal', a sigh.*

We watch as she tries to enjoy her breakfast.

After the food is gone she fills a glass of water. As she sips it, she notices her hand reaching for something — something more to eat.

TIGHT ON *the kitchen clock ticking real slow. Her Timex the same.*

We see her eyes, her lips, her twitching fingers.

A quick glimpse at the fridge. She grabs her stomach and says to it:

Stop already.

(*then to herself*)

You'll feel better in the red dress than a cheese danish.

CUT TO:

INT. MARION'S BATHROOM

Marion throws some cold water on her face. She looks at her naked body in the mirror. She feels lifeless, drab and dead.

QUICK CUTS: *Tinfoil crinkles, powder sprinkles, lighter flicks, smoke drifts, straw sucks, a pleasant sigh . . .*

Once again, Marion looks in the mirror.

Now she looks alive and glorious. Rays of golden light encase her body in a gentle glow.

She cups her hands under her breasts and smiles as she turns and poses, admiring their size and firmness.

'Not bad,' she thinks.

CUT TO:

INT. SARA'S MAILBOX – DAY

Nothing.

CUT TO:

INT. SARA'S APARTMENT

Sara tries to watch TV but the fridge beckons her.

TIGHT ON *the kitchen clock, slowly, slowly ticking.*

The fridge shudders. Frustrated, Sara grabs her folding chair and heads out.

CUT TO:

EXT. SARA'S BUILDING — DAY

The outside of the building is lined with the old Yentas *sitting in beach chairs catching the sun. A few have reflectors and stare up at the sun.*

Sara exits her building and lets the sun hit her hair. Her friend Rae says something first.

                    RAE
Ada told us. It's gorgeous.

                    SARA
Thank you. We're making it a little darker tomorrow.

                    RAE
So why darker?

                    SARA
To match my red dress.

                    RAE
But now it's looking like Lucille Ball.

                    SARA
But I'm not. But soon . . . I'm on a diet.

ADA

Yes, she is.

YENTA #1

Cottage cheese and lettuce?

ADA

No.

RAE

What diet you on?

SARA

Eggs and grapefruit.

RAE

Oi vay. I was on that once. Lots of luck, Dolly.

SARA

It's not so bad.

RAE

How long you been on already?

SARA

All day.

RAE

All day? It's one o'clock.

SARA

So, I'm thinking thin.

Now, old Mrs Scarlini pipes up.

MRS SCARLINI

My Rosie lost fifty pounds like that almost.

YENTA #1

Like that?

SARA

Like what?

MRS SCARLINI

Poof.

RAE

You put her in a sweat box?

MRS SCARLINI

A doctor. He gave her pills. It makes you not want to eat.

YENTA #1

So what's so good about that? You mean I'm sitting here not thinking about chopped liver and pastrami on rye?

MRS SCARLINI

With a slice of onion and mustard.

YENTA #2

Herring.

YENTA #1

Herring?

YENTA#2

Yeah, herring. In sour cream. When the sun goes behind the building I'm having a nosh.

ADA

You shouldn't talk like that when someone's on a diet.

SARA

Eh, big deal. I'll sneak an extra piece of lettuce. I'm thinking thin.

RAE

The mailman . . .

Just then, the Mailman arrives. Sara picks up her chair and follows him into the building. Ada, Rae and the other Yentas *follow Sara.*

SARA

Goldfarb. Goldfarb. I know you have something for Goldfarb.

MAILMAN

Let's see. Not much around here except at the beginning of the month with the social security checks.

SARA

But I'm expecting something –

MAILMAN

Here we go. Something for Goldfarb, Sara Goldfarb.

He hands her a thick manila envelope.

CUT TO:

INT. SARA'S APARTMENT

The Yentas *follow Sara into the apartment.* Yenta #2 *flips on the TV, someone else starts a pot of coffee.*

ADA

So let's see.

YENTA #1

Open it, open it.

Sara carefully opens the envelope. She takes out a questionnaire.

RAE

So when do you go on?

SARA

They decide after you send this form.

ADA

Oh, it's so exciting.

The other women murmur their excitement, too. Ada takes the application from Sara and places it on the table.

OK, OK. You sit, Dolly and just answer the questions.

Sara, a bit nervous, sits down. Ada gives her a pencil and leans over her shoulder. The Yentas *crowd around.*

Name? Easy enough. S-a-r-a G-o-l-d-f-a-r-b.

SARA

You call that a question? That kind I take six at once.

The Yentas *laugh as Sara carefully prints her name.*

ADA

Address.

31

SARA

A breeze.

Sara fills out question after question until:

ADA

Uh-oh.

SARA

What? What?

ADA

Date of Birth.

SARA

So now you're getting personal. OK, I'll tell you.

She fills it in.

ADA

Age?

SARA

So now you want me to count for you!

ADA

Marital Status?

SARA
(*smiles*)

Wanting, needing. How about if I win Robert Redford?

A big laugh.

ADA

Sex?

A bigger laugh.

SARA

Please?

The biggest.

ADA

That's it, Dolly.

Sara holds the paper against her chest and says a short prayer. The Yentas *respect her silence.*

Then she carefully folds it and places it in the self-addressed envelope. She seals it and holds the flap down for many seconds.

Then she puts it on her chair and sits on it, just to make sure it's sealed.

Next she tosses her head and shoulders at the refrigerator and says to it:

> SARA
>
> Who needs you?

CUT TO:

EXT. SARA'S BUILDING – A MOMENT LATER

Sara marches out of the building waving the envelope. The Yentas *follow their friend. Victorious, they march to the mailbox.*

> YENTA #1
>
> I wonder when you'll hear?

> ADA
>
> Maybe they'll send you to Tavern on the Green, that's where they send all the stars.

SARA

I'm eating eggs and grapefruit at Tavern on the Green.

The ladies laugh as they follow their hero, their savior, their victor. Suddenly, the envelope begins to glow. It glows a brilliant white.

At the mailbox Sara kisses the envelope and drops it in the mail slot. She closes the lid and then opens it to make sure it has dropped into the box.

And then the ladies huddle around Sara as the blue mailbox begins to radiate and bathe them in a cool blue light. The Yentas *'ooooh' and 'ahhh'.*

CUT TO:

INT. TYRONE'S DIVE PAD

Tyrone is on the phone with Brody's Henchman. Harry sits at the table counting twenties into a small, neat pile.

TYRONE

Dynamite? Dynamite. Dynamite! Alright, we's on the way.

Tyrone hangs up.

Brody's man says it's real fine shit.

HARRY

Alright. Here we go.

TYRONE

Here we go.

HARRY
(*serious*)

Let's do this right.

TYRONE

Naturally.

Tyrone takes the money and slaps Harry five. Exit Tyrone.

Harry spins some vinyl, rolls a joint, sparks it and takes a few pokes. He starts grooving with the music as his nervousness dissolves.

Then something is off and Harry feels it. He stops the turntable.

Suddenly, it's a sunny day in Tyrone's bedroom. The back wall is gone and stretching into the sea is –

THE CONEY ISLAND PIER

Now, strolling with a baby carriage is a woman in a red dress. It's Marion.

Harry watches her from Tyrone's apartment.

He calls for her but she keeps going. He chases after her.

He's trying to get a glimpse into the carriage. Finally, Marion hears him and she spins around. She smiles and waves.

She reaches into the carriage to pick something up. Harry is almost with her. He keeps running.

And just as he's about to get a peek, he stops. He hears a key in a lock.

He spins round and we –

CUT BACK TO:

INT. TYRONE'S DIVE PAD – NOW

Tyrone enters the room with a big-ass, shit-eatin' grin on his face.

He drops a little package on the table.

TYRONE

There it is, Jim.

HARRY

Huh?

TYRONE

There it is.

Harry snaps out of it and he looks at the package.

Shall we try?

HARRY

Wait, Ty. This is our chance to make it big and I mean really big. We don't have to be dealin' in no petty-ass pieces all our lives. We play it right an' we can get a pound of pure, but if we get wasted we'll fuck it up.

TYRONE

Right, on, baby, ahm not jivin' you. Ah doan' want to be runnin' no streets the res' of mah life in no ripped sneakers, mah nose runnin' down to mah chin. All we gotta do is have a little taste so we know how much to cut it.

HARRY

Fair enough.

Palms slap, then: flick, sizzle, snap, suck, slap, rush, sigh . . .

And: flick, sizzle, snap, suck, slap, rush, sigh . . .

Tyrone and Harry look at each other with flush faces and hanging heads.

They grin at each other.

TYRONE

Sheeit . . .

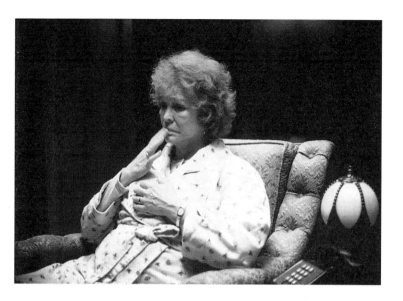

Then they laugh and laugh and laugh.

CUT TO:

EXT. BOARDWALK – DAY

Marion sits in front of the Wonder Wheel watching the summer crowd play.

She unpacks the shopping bag next to her. She pulls out some sketch pads, pencils, charcoal and a sharpener.

She stares at the blank page. A moment later, she begins to sketch.

CUT TO:

INT. SARA'S APARTMENT

Sara sits in her chair trying to watch TV.

But she can't concentrate. The kitchen clock ticks terribly slowly. So does her Timex.

Everywhere she looks in the room steaming hot food appears. Over there, by her plants, is a bacon doublecheese burger. Then over there, by the lamp, is a chocolate-covered eclair.

She grabs a glass of water and downs it.

She turns to the fridge. It shudders at her. She screams at it:

SARA

Shut up!

Suddenly the fridge door becomes transparent. She can see all the produce in her stuffed fridge beckoning her.

She turns away and goes into –

THE BEDROOM

She flips off the light and tries to sleep.

She closes her eyes but they pop open. Then slowly her beige ceiling disappears and turns into a clear blue sky with puffy, white clouds. Then it dissolves into a sizzling, juicy pizza-pie.

Sara twists and turns. Then the pie turns into a chocolate-covered cherry. Then it becomes a bagel smothered with lox, onions and crowned with a healthy slice of tomato.

There's no hope. Sara sits up in her bed and reaches for the phone. She dials.

MRS SCARLINI
(*off-screen*)

Hello?

SARA

Louise, it's Sara. I need the number of that doctor.

CUT TO:

INT. MARION'S APARTMENT

ON *Harry looking hollow.*

HARRY

Why do you have to see him for krist's sake? Cut the son of a bitch loose.

Marion is dressing herself up in front of the mirror. She looks like a million bucks in a chic black dress. She carefully applies her lipstick.

I don't want him mentioning to my parents that I have stopped therapy. They're already pissed at me and they're thinking of cutting me off.

Marion turns and touches Harry's face tenderly.

Sweetheart, I am not going to sleep with him. He's got some issue with womanly blood so I told him I'm on the rag. He's planning on going home after the concert.

Harry tries not to sulk, but his chin dips. Then Marion chuckles but Harry doesn't respond. Suddenly, she hugs him and squeals with absolute glee.

Oh Harry, you're jealous!

Harry half-heartedly tries to push her away but Marion doesn't let him.

Come on, sweetheart, put your arms around me, come on, please!? Please!?

She lifts his hands and puts them on her shoulders as she snuggles deeper into him. Then she starts kissing him on the ears, eyelids and neck and soon he starts to giggle.

HARRY

Come on, stop, stop you crazy girl or I'll bite you on the throat.

They laugh as they tickle each other and cover each other in kisses.

CUT TO:

INT. RAOUL'S CAFE – NIGHT

A fancy French pretension – two plates of frogs' legs, two glasses of Cinzano with twists, and a stunning Marion with a dumpy Arnold the Shrink.

ARNOLD THE SHRINK

I'm disappointed that you are indisposed.

MARION

Is Anita out of town or something?

ARNOLD THE SHRINK

Why do you ask?

MARION

I'm just curious if she's 'indisposed'.

ARNOLD THE SHRINK
(*taken aback*)

Marion. No she's fine.

MARION

Can I ask you something personal, Arnold?

ARNOLD THE SHRINK

What is it?

Arnold leans in. Then she fucks with him. She tells him he's got something on his face when he doesn't. She tortures him until all she can do is laugh.

CUT TO:

EXT. PROJECTS – NIGHT

Sodium streetlight pops as Tyrone cold lamps by a beat-up bodega.

A black hand slaps Tyrone money. The money slides into his pocket. Tyrone's eyes swish left then right. He slips something out from behind the tire of a parked car. And slaps a bag of white powder back.

Pop, slap, slide, swish, slip, slap! Again. And again. And again.

CUT TO:

EXT. OTHER SIDE OF THE PROJECTS – NIGHT

Neon crackle as Harry chills outside an OTB.

A white hand slaps Harry money. The money slips into his pocket. Harry's eyes swish right then left. He clinks something out of a trash can. And he slaps a bag of white powder back.

Crackle, slap, slip, swish, clink, slap! Again. And again. And again.

CUT TO:

INT. MARION'S APARTMENT – LATER

Harry spins Marion around.

> **HARRY**
> We're on our way, baby, we're really on our way.

> **MARION**
> Harry.

> **HARRY**
> It was great out there. Everyone's thirsty.

> **MARION**
> I'm so glad. And baby, I'm drawing again. I'm drawing. I can't stop.

Marion takes out her sketchbook. She shows him her sketches.

Harry and Marion lean into each other, suddenly hugging each other, kissing, dreaming and believing.

CUT TO:

INT. DOCTOR PILL'S EXAMINING ROOM

A Skinny Nurse weighs and measures Sara.

SKINNY NURSE

How are you?

SARA

Fine, that's why I'm here.

They both laugh. The Nurse takes Sara's blood pressure.

SKINNY NURSE

How's your hearing and vision?

SARA

I have both.

The Nurse laughs again.

SKINNY NURSE

Now, wait just a minute.

The nurse smiles and leaves.

A moment later, Doctor Pill enters. He looks at the chart the Nurse filled out and then he smiles at Sara.

DOCTOR PILL

I see you're a little overweight.

SARA

A little? I have fifty pounds I'm willing to donate.

DOCTOR PILL

We can take care of that, no problem.

CUT TO:

HIP-HOT MINI-MONTAGE

TIGHTS *of dope being cut, plastic bags being filled, Tyrone and Harry dealing, Marion sketching and sewing, Harry and Marion kissing, Harry spinning tunes, flick, sizzle, snap, suck, slap, rush, sigh and crinkle, sprinkle, flick, drift, suck, sigh . . .*

CUT TO:

INT. TYRONE'S CLOSET

Harry and Tyrone neatly stuff a shoe box full of money. They put a rubber band around the box and hide it in the back of the closet.

Harry gives Tyrone five, Tyrone gives Harry five.

CUT TO:

INT. EMPTY STORE – DAY

In photographs, a straight Real Estate Agent shows Harry and Marion around the empty store.

OUTSIDE

The Agent snaps a photo of the lovers in front of the store.

CUT TO:

INT. SARA'S KITCHEN

On the table in front of her are four bottles of pills and the instructions.

> SARA
> Purple in the morning. Red in the afternoon. Orange in the evening.
> *(to the refrigerator)*
> That's my three meals, Mr Smarty Pants.
> *(then to herself)*
> Green at night. Just like that. One, two, three, four . . .

She pops a purple: a pill cap pops off, pill hits hand, mouth gulps, pill cap snaps on.

Then she heads to the fridge and makes herself a smoked fish and cream cheese sandwich on an onion Kaiser roll.

She shows off to the fridge as she devours it.

Then she makes a cup of coffee: an empty pot tinkles into place, the coffee perks, the coffee drips, and then Sara slurps, slurps, slurps.

She picks up the remote and flips on the set but she can't seem to sit down, so she heads outside with her chair.

CUT TO:

INT. SARA'S MAILBOX – DAY

Sara peeks in for anything – nothing.

CUT TO:

INT. CONEY ISLAND ARCADE

Marion and Harry play skeeball. Marion hits a fifty and smiles. Harry stops playing.

> HARRY
>
> Yeah, that's what I'll do.

> MARION
>
> Huh?

> HARRY
>
> For my mom. I've been thinking of getting something for her, you know, some kind of present, but I didn't know what to get.

> MARION
>
> Well?

> HARRY
>
> I finally asked myself, what's her fix? Television, right? If ever there's a TV junkie it's the old lady. I figure maybe I owe her a new one anyway with all the wear and tear her set got from being schlepped back and forth to old Abe's.

> MARION
>
> You really love her, don't you?

> HARRY
>
> I don't know. I guess so. One time I feel one way and the other time I feel something else. Most of the time I just want her to be happy.

> MARION
>
> Let's go get it now.

44

HARRY

Well . . .

MARION

C'mon.

HARRY

I don't wanna deal with salesmen . . .

MARION

Oh, come on.

HARRY
(*gets an idea*)

Well, let's push off first.

MARION

It's still early. We shouldn't get going till tonight.

HARRY

Yeah, I know, but this is different. After all, I was always usin'
the old lady's set to cop money so now we'll use a little stuff
to get her a set.

Marion doesn't fight him.

Then there's the: flick, sizzle, snap, suck, slap, rush, sigh . . .

And: crinkle, sprinkle, flick, drift, suck, sigh . . .

CUT TO:

INT. SARA'S APARTMENT

Coffee: tinkle, perk, drip, slurp, slurp, slurp . . .

and

Pill: pop, hit, gulp, snap . . .

Sara starts to clean the apartment.

Time races by as she intricately cleans every single square inch of the kitchen. She cleans the inside of the fridge and dumps all the food.

Next, she moves into the living room and continues to clean.

Then everything slows down.

Sara collapses into her viewing chair in front of the TV. She tries to watch but she's squirming in her seat.

Then she notices something wrong. She's not sure what so she heads into –

THE BATHROOM

In the mirror, she stares at her clenched teeth grinding. She wonders what this means. She shrugs and takes the green pill: pop, hit, gulp, snap . . .

BACK IN THE LIVING ROOM

– Sara sits in front of the TV and watches Tappy Tibbons preach. Slowly she dozes off.

CUT TO:

INT. TYRONE'S DIVE PAD

Tyrone's old pad has been spruced up. It's filled with tons of cool toys. It looks like Christmas morning.

Beautiful and very young Alice lies naked in the giant bed staring at Tyrone.

He sits naked at his desk playing with flip books. First there's a wacky duck dancing, then there's a crying GI soldier.

ALICE
Why dontcha come back to bed, honey?

TYRONE
Sheeit, plenty time for that, woman, I got me a cool-ass toy ahm groovin' behind.

Tyrone picks up another flip book and lets things rip. The animation suddenly turns into live action and we are following the back of a little boy.

The boy runs across a black room into the arms of a beautiful woman.

The boy is Young Tyrone and the woman is Tyrone's Mother.

YOUNG TYRONE
I told ya, Ma. One day I'd make it.

TYRONE'S MOTHER
You don't have to make anything. You just gotta love your momma.

The image of boy and mother dies when the flip book ends. Tyrone looks at it sadly.

ALICE
What are you doing, honey?

TYRONE
Thinking about you, baby, and what I'm gonna do to ya.

Tyrone leaps onto the bed and Alice squeals playfully.

ALICE
Don't do that, Tyrone. You'll scare me to death.

TYRONE
Oh little momma, I wouldn't want to scare you . . . I doan' want to scare nobody. All I want from life is no hassles and some peace and harmony . . . an' I want it from the finest fox that ever lived.

CUT TO:

INT. SARA'S MAILBOX – DAY

Still empty . . .

CUT TO:

INT. SARA'S BUILDING – DAY

Pop, hit, gulp, snap and tinkle, perk, drip, slurp, slurp, slurp . . .

The Yentas *all rise when Sara comes out and they move their chairs so that she can have her proper seat in the sun.*

                    YENTA #1
Sara, you know yet when?

                    YENTA #2
Are you hearing anything?

                         SARA
Nothing yet.

                         ADA
You can bring friends?

                         SARA
How should I know?

                         ADA
They should let you bring at least a schlepper. Who's going to carry home all those prizes?

                         SARA
Believe me, I'll get them home. Especially Robert Redford. For him I don't need a schlepper.

But Sara is having a hard time sitting still. She looks up and down the street for the Mailman and paces around her friends.

They watch her with a bit of concern. Then Mrs Scarlini comes out of the building for sunning. Sara grabs her and hugs her.

   I love you forever. I can't believe it but I'm not even thinking

48

of food. If you put down a big bowl of chicken noodle soup I wouldn't eat it. Thank you so much, Rosie. Thank you!

CUT TO:

INT. TYRONE'S NEW PAD

Alice and Tyrone make some crazy love. Arms flail, teeth bite, mouths scream. Some crazy love.

CUT TO:

INT. SARA'S APARTMENT

Sara stands in front of the mirror trying on the red dress. The dress won't close.

Pop, hit, gulp, snap . . .

The red dress gets a little closer.

Pop, hit, gulp, snap . . .

The dress gets even closer.

CUT TO:

INT. TAXI CAB – MOVING

Harry squirms in the back seat wearing a sharp new pair of slacks, a sports shirt and a pair of new shoes.

He nervously pats down his hair and adjusts his collar.

CUT TO:

EXT. SARA'S BUILDING

The Yentas *all admire Sara's slim figure until the Mailman approaches. Everyone turns to him – hoping . . .*

He grins and shakes his head.

MAILMAN
When I see it I'll be waving it all over the place.

The Mailman enters the building.

A cab pulls up. Harry steps out. He stares at the intimidating line of Yentas.

Sara stares for a brief second not computing this apparition.

Then she jumps up and wraps her arms around him, almost knocking him off balance.

> SARA

Harry!

She kisses him and he kisses her. She's so excited she kisses him again.

> HARRY

Hey, take it easy, Ma, you'll crush me.

He gives her a quick smile as he adjusts his clothes.

> SARA

Come, come inside, Harry. I'll make you a pot of coffee and we'll have a visit.

She grabs his hand and heads to the entrance.

CUT TO:

INT. SARA'S APARTMENT

Sara makes a pot of coffee as she bustles around grabbing cups, saucers, spoons, milk and napkins.

Harry stares wide-eyed at his hyperactive mother. He tries to get a word in but can't.

> SARA

And how are you, Harry, you're looking so good. You want something to eat?

> HARRY

No, Ma –

> SARA

A little nosh, maybe, or cake, I'll go get some if you want, but I don't have anything in the house but Ada will have something, a cupcake, maybe.

HARRY

No –

Finally, the coffee is ready and she fills two cups.

SARA
You want something to eat?

HARRY
(*almost screams*)
No, Ma. Nothing. Sit. Sit, for krist's sake. You're making me dizzy.

SARA
You notice something? You notice I'm slimmer?

HARRY
Yeah, yeah, I guess you are, Mom.

SARA
Twenty-five pounds. You believe it? Twenty-five pounds and that's just the beginning.

HARRY

That's great, Ma. That's really great, I'm really happy for ya. But sit down, eh?

Sara sits, Harry is bewildered.

I'm sorry I haven't been around for awhile, Ma, but I've been busy, real busy.

Sara nods as she clenches her jaw.

SARA

You got yourself a good job? You're doing well?

HARRY

Yeah, Ma, real good.

SARA

What kind of business?

HARRY

Well, I'm sort of a distributor, like. For a big importer. My own.

SARA

Oh, I'm so happy for you.

Sara gets up and smothers Harry with kisses.

HARRY

Hey, Ma, easy, eh? You're killing me. Krist, whatta ya been doin', liftin' weights?

SARA

Your own business. Oh Harry, I knew when I saw you that you had your own business. I always knew that you could do that.

HARRY
(*smiles*)

Yeah, Ma, you were right. I made it just like you said I would.

SARA

So now maybe you'll meet a nice girl and have a baby?

HARRY

I already met one –

Sara squeals and squeaks and starts to jump out of her chair. Harry holds his arms up in front of him.

Jesus krist, Ma, don't go ape shit, eh?

SARA

Is she a nice girl? Who's her parents? What –

HARRY

You know'er, Ma. Marion. Marion Silver. Remember, they –

SARA

Oh, Silver. Of course. I know Manhattan Beach. He's got a house on the esplanade. Garment business.

HARRY

Yeah, yeah, he's big in women's undies.

Harry chuckles. Sara is so happy, she can't stay sitting. She refills their cups.

Before you go bouncin' all over again and make me forget, what I want to tell ya is I got you a present and –

SARA

Harry, I don't want a present, just have a baby.

HARRY

Later for that, eh? Will you let me tell you what I got, eh? Will ya?

Sara nods, grins, grinds and clenches.

Krist, you're really something else today. Look, I know . . . well . . .
              (*deep breath*)
What I'm trying to say is that . . . well . . .
              (*shrugs*)
Well . . . I know I ain't been the best son in the world –

SARA

Oh, Harry, you're a good –

HARRY

No, no! Please, Ma, let me finish. I'll never get it out if you keep interrupting me.

(*deep breath*)

I'm sorry for being such a bastard.

(*stop – breathe – sigh*)

I wanna make it up. I mean, I know I can't change anything that's happened, but I want ya to know that I'm sorry and I love ya, and I wanna make it right.

SARA

Harry, it's –

HARRY

I don't know why I do those things. I don't really want to do them. It just sort've happens, I guess. I don't know. It's all kinda goofy somehow, but I really do love ya, Ma, and I want you to be happy so I got ya a brand new TV set. It's gonna be delivered in a couple a days. From Macy's.

Sara squeals, but Harry wards her off with his hands. She sits down, grins and grinds her teeth.

SARA

Oh, Harry, you're such a good boy. Your father would be so happy to see what you're doing for your poor, lonely mother.

Harry leans over and gives her an honest, open and perfectly beautiful kiss.

You see that, Seymour? You see how good your son is? He knows how lonely his mother is living all alone, no one to make her a visit . . .

Harry feels pretty good as he listens to his mother until something puzzles him. He stops hearing his mother and now he suddenly hears some other, strange sound. What is it?

He looks around until he looks at his mother. Suddenly he is filled with surprise, disbelief and confusion.

The noise he hears is his mother's teeth grinding.

54

TIGHT ON *Sara's mouth. Harry leans across the table.*

> **HARRY**
>
> Hey, Ma, you droppin' uppers?

> **SARA**
>
> What?

> **HARRY**
>
> You on uppers?
> *(getting angry)*
> You're on diet pills, ain't ya?

Sara is suddenly stunned. She's completely bewildered.

> **SARA**
>
> On? On? What is on?

> **HARRY**
>
> How come ya lost so much weight?

> **SARA**
>
> I told you, I'm going to a specialist.

> **HARRY**
>
> A specialist. What kinda specialist?

> **SARA**
>
> What kind? A specialist. For weight.

> **HARRY**
>
> Yeah, that's what I thought. You're makin' a croaker for speed, ain't ya?

> **SARA**
>
> Harry, you alright?
> *(shrugs)*
> I'm just going to a doctor. I don't know from croaker, making –

> **HARRY**
>
> What does he give ya, Ma? Eh? Does he give ya pills?

> **SARA**
>
> Of course he gives me pills. He's a doctor. Doctors give pills.

HARRY

What kind of pills?

SARA

What kind. A purple one, red one, orange and –

HARRY

No, no, I mean what kind?

SARA

They're round . . . and flat.

HARRY
(*rolls eyes*)

I mean, like what's in them?

SARA

Harry, I'm Sara Goldfarb, not Albert Einstein. How should I know what's in them?

HARRY

Look, Ma, does that stuff make you feel good sort of and give you lots of pep?

SARA
(*nods*)

Well, I guess maybe a little.

HARRY

A little? Jesus, I can hear ya grinding ya teeth from here.

SARA

But that goes away at night.

HARRY

At night?

SARA

When I take the green one. In thirty minutes I'm asleep. Poof, just like that.

Harry shakes his head and rolls his eyes.

HARRY

Hey, Ma, ya gotta cut that stuff loose. It's no good.

SARA

Who said it's no good? Twenty-five pounds I lost.

HARRY

Big deal. Do ya wanna be a dope fiend fa krist's sake?

SARA

What's this dope fiend? Am I foaming at the mouth? He's a nice doctor.

HARRY

Ma, I'm telling ya this croaker's no good.

SARA

How come you know so much? How come you know more about medicine than a doctor?

HARRY

(*deep sigh*)

I know, Ma, believe me, I know. You'll get strung out fa krist's sake.

SARA

C'mon. I almost fit in my red dress, the one I wore at your high school graduation. The one your father liked so much. I remember how he looked at me in the red dress. It's not long after that he got sick and died and you're without a father, my poor baby, but thank God he saw you happy for a little and –

HARRY

What's with the red dress? What does that –

SARA

I'm going to wear the red dress on . . . Oh, you don't know. I'm going to be on television. I got a call and an application and –

HARRY

C'mon, Ma, who's pullin' ya leg?

SARA

I'm telling you I'm being a contestant on television. They haven't told me when, but you'll see, you'll be proud when you see your mother in her red dress and golden shoes on television.

What's the big deal about being on television? Those pills'll kill ya before ya ever get on, fa krist's sake.

SARA

Big deal? You drove up in a cab. You see who had the sun seat? You notice your mother in the special spot getting the sun? You know who everybody talks to? You know who's somebody now? Who's no longer just a widow in a little apartment who lives alone? I'm somebody now, Harry. Everyone likes me. Soon millions of people will see me and like me. I'll tell them about you and your father. I'll tell them how your father liked the red dress and how good he was to us. Remember?

Harry nods. Defeated, he stares at the floor.

And who knows what I might win? A new refrigerator. A Rolls-Royce, maybe. Robert Redford.

HARRY

Robert Redford?

SARA

So what's wrong with Robert Redford?

Harry blinks and shakes his head. Bewildered, he surrenders to her flow.

Sara looks at her entire family and a softness overtakes her.

It's not the prizes, Harry. It doesn't make any difference if I win or lose. It's like a reason to get up in the morning. It's a reason to lose weight so I can be healthy. It's a reason to fit in the red dress. It's a reason to smile, already. It makes tomorrow alright.

(*close to Harry now*)

What have I got, Harry? Why should I even make the bed or wash the dishes? I do them, but why should I? I'm alone. Seymour's gone, you're gone, I have no one to take care of. Anybody. Everybody. What do I have? I'm lonely, Harry. I'm old.

Harry fidgets, his eyes blink, he tries:

HARRY

You got friends, Ma. What –

SARA

It's not the same. You need someone to make for. No, Harry, I like how I feel this way. I like thinking about the red dress and the television . . . and your father and you. Now when I get the sun I smile.

HARRY

I'll come visit, Ma. Now that I'm straight, my business is going good, I'll come. Me and Marion. Honest, Ma. I swear. We'll come for dinner. Soon.

Sara shakes her head and smiles at Harry, trying hard to believe.

SARA

Good, you bring her and I'll make your soup and a roast.

HARRY

That sounds great, Ma. I'll give you a call ahead a time, OK?

SARA
(nods)

Good. I'm glad. I'm glad you got a nice girl and a good business. I'm glad.

Sara gets up and hugs Harry, tears welling in her eyes.

Your father and I were always wanting only the very best for you. I'm glad, Harry, that you have someone to be with. You should be healthy and happy. And have lots of babies. Don't have only one. It's no good. Have lots of babies. They'll make you happy.

Harry does his best to hug his mother. He fights his desperation to get away and holds onto her.

Eventually, Sara backs away and looks into his face, smiling.

Look, I'm crying already. I'm so happy I'm crying.

                              HARRY
                         (*forces smiles*)
      I'm glad you're happy, Ma. I really love ya. An' I'm sorry –

Sara waves his apologies away – tosh, tosh.

      I really am. But I'm goin' ta make it up now. You should just
      be happy.

                              SARA
      Don't worry about me. I'm used to being alone.

*A long silent beat as child and parent smile at each other. Harry looks
at his watch.*

                              HARRY
      I got to go, Ma. I have an appointment in Manhattan in a
      little bit. But I'll be back.

                              SARA
      Good. I'll make for you. You still have your key?

                              HARRY
                         (*shows her*)
      Yeah, I got it, Ma. I'd better hurry. I'm late now.

                              SARA
      Goodbye, Son.

*One more kiss and hug and Harry is gone. Sara stares at the door for
many long moments.*

*Then she takes her orange pill – pop, hit, gulp, snap – and washes it
down with a fresh cup of coffee.*

CUT TO:

INT. MOVING CAB

*Harry sits in the back seat filled with worry and concern. Tears well up
into his eyes until he can't hold it any longer. He sobs hard, real hard.*

*A moment later he collects himself and gets high: flick, sizzle, snap,
suck, slap, rush, sigh . . .*

Harry wipes away his tears.

                               60

CUT TO:

INT. SARA'S BEDROOM

Sara zips up the red dress. It closes.

She swings around gloriously and her locked jaw smiles at herself in the mirror. Eyes glow.

And she begins to waltz by herself. Humming . . .

HARD CUT TO:

BLACK

ON THE SCREEN IN WHITE LETTERS: 'FALL'

CUT TO:

INT. BRODY'S LIMO

Tyrone steps into a white limo with leopardskin upholstery.

He exchanges fives with, Brody (late twenties, bespectacled, highly intelligent looking) and his two Henchmen.

Brody doesn't speak. He signs to Henchman #1

> HENCHMAN
> Brody say you coming up quick, kid.

> TYRONE
> Thanks, Brody.

The Henchman signs back. Then Brody responds.

> HENCHMAN
> Brody wants to promote you. He wants to give you some more responsibility. Are you interested?

> TYRONE
> Yeah, yeah.

> HENCHMAN
> Brody say, you fuck him, I'll kill you.

TYRONE

I wouldn't do that, Jim.

Just then, Tyrone notices the driver's door is open. Tyrone points.

Where's the –

Brody spins just when a White Gunman leans in through the driver's door with a 9mm Glock –

BANG! BANG! BANG!

Three bullets rip through Brody's body. Blood and guts splatter Tyrone and Brody's dead body collapses into his lap.

The Henchmen pull out their pieces and return fire. One Henchman gets splattered. The other kills the White Man.

Tyrone slips and scrambles out of the limo. The White Gunman lies dead in the street.

Tyrone runs! Frantic, with blood all over him, he runs hyperventilating with panic until two Cops give chase. Sirens and lights.

They catch him and slam him against the wall. Cuff wrist one, cuff wrist two.

CUT TO:

INT. SARA'S APARTMENT

Pop, hit, gulp, snap . . .

Sara's living room is dominated by a gigantic, towering, black TV. The ominous hulk of technology stares down on Sara who sits in her lazy chair staring at the set's cold, dark screen.

Something is wrong.

Some coffee: tinkle, perk, drip, slurp, slurp, slurp . . .

Nothing. So one more:

Pop, hit, gulp, snap . . .

CUT TO:

INT. MARION'S APARTMENT

Flick, sizzle, snap, suck, slap, rush, sigh . . .

Crinkle, sprinkle, flick, drift, suck, sigh . . .

Harry and Marion lean against each other on the floor. They stare up at the ceiling. Sketches and pieces of Marion's clothing lie around them.

> MARION
> Oh Harry, I love you. You make me feel like a person, like I'm me and I'm beautiful.

> HARRY
> You are beautiful. You're the most beautiful woman in the world. You're my dream.

CUT TO:

INT. SARA'S APARTMENT

Pop, hit, gulp, snap . . .

Sara still sits. She feels nothing.

Coffee: tinkle, perk, drip, slurp, slurp, slurp . . .

Still nothing.

She picks up the bottles of pills from Doctor Pill and examines the labels.

She looks real close.

Then she calls Doctor Pill.

> SKINNY NURSE
> (*off-screen*)
> Doctor's office?

> SARA
> Hello, this is Mrs Goldfarb –

> SKINNY NURSE
> (*off-screen*)
> No, Mrs Goldfarb, I'm absolutely certain. I've checked again.

SARA

Are you sure you didn't give me the wrong pills?

SKINNY NURSE
(*off-screen*)

No.

SARA

But maybe you gave me a smaller one the last time.

SKINNY NURSE
(*off-screen*)

That isn't possible, Mrs Goldfarb. You see, they are all the same potency. The change is in the color. All the purple are the same strength, all the red, etc.

SARA

But something isn't the same.

SKINNY NURSE
(*off-screen*)

You're just becoming adjusted to them. At first you get a strong reaction, but after a while that wears off and you just don't feel like eating. It's nothing to worry about, Mrs Goldfarb.

Click. Sara stares at the phone and slowly hangs it up.

She drops two pills in her hand. She stares at both pills – shrugs and pops them: pop, hit, gulp, snap . . .

Then a small grin invades her face. Something's happening.

She flips on the TV to Tappy:

TAPPY TIBBONS

Now let's meet our next winner. She's a beautiful woman with a winning sense of humor and a magical smile. Straight from Brighton Beach, Brooklyn, let's give a juicy welcome to Mrs Sara Goldfarb.

And there she is! Red, red, red. Sara smiles at Red Sara. The audience loves her.

Juice by Sara! Juice by Sara! Juice by Sara! ooooOOOOH!
Sara's got juice! Sara's got juice! ooooOOOH Sara!

*But back in the real world, the fridge shudders. Sara stares at it,
concerned.*

CUT TO:

INT. HOLDING TANK — NIGHT

*Tyrone, terrified, holds onto the bars for dear life. Junkies and winos
that seem more like ghosts and giant rats taunt him. Until:*

> GUARD
> (*off-screen*)
> Love . . . Love, Tyrone C. Seven-three-five. Get your shit
> together and come on.

CUT TO:

EXT. CONEY ISLAND STREET — MOVING

*Harry and Tyrone rap as they scam the streets searching for a
connection. They eye other junkies suspiciously.*

> TYRONE

How much?

> HARRY

They got most of our cash. You're up for consortin'.

> TYRONE

Sheeit.

> HARRY

Angel says it's a war between the Italians and the Blacks. He
says Sal the Geep is keeping all the shit down in Florida until
guys like Brody are all knocked off.

> TYRONE

Sheeit.

> HARRY

No one's got a thing.

                              TYRONE
Except Big Tim.

                              HARRY
Who?

                              TYRONE
He's holdin' a nice taste.

                              HARRY
How much?

                              TYRONE
Some say a piece, others a truckload.

                              HARRY
Shit. Let's go see him.

                              TYRONE
He's holdin', but he's not sellin'. He's only givin' up for
pussy.

                              HARRY
What?

                              TYRONE
The only habit that muthafuck have is pussy. He hooked on
that thang. Ah told'im ah give'im all he want, but he say ahm
not pretty enough for'im.

*Just then, a white van screeches to a halt at the corner in front of them.
The side door slides open. Two white guys toss a dead black guy into a
city garbage can.*

The van screeches off. The black guy's sneakers poke up out of the can.

Harry and Tyrone turn around and quickly exit the scene.

CUT TO:

INT. MARION'S APARTMENT

                              MARION
Well, why don't we just stop using?

Harry, Tyrone and Marion stare at each other for a moment, the

implication of Marion's question slowly, through much resistance, sinking in and registering.

HARRY

Yeah, I guess we'd better.

CUT TO:

INT. SARA'S MAILBOX

Still nothing.

CUT TO:

INT. SARA'S APARTMENT

Pop, hit, gulp, snap . . .

Sara starts to circle around the lazy chair. Tighter and tighter circles.

CUT TO:

INT. MARION'S APARTMENT

We pan the apartment and see Harry, Tyrone and Marion trying to do something, anything but nothing. But everything is real slow and every moment is real painful.

The kitchen clock is almost moving backwards. We see their eyes. Their sweating lips. Their twitching fingers.

CUT TO:

INT. SARA'S MAILBOX

Nope

CUT TO:

INT. SARA'S APARTMENT

Pop, hit, gulp, snap – and again – pop, hit, gulp, snap . . .

Sara stops pacing. Out of breath, she towers over the phone. She dials 411. Her mouth races after her speed-drenched mind.

>   COMPUTERIZED OPERATOR
>   (off-screen)
> Welcome to Bell Atlantic. Number please?

>   SARA
> Malin & Block. Manhattan.

>   COMPUTERIZED OPERATOR
>   (off-screen)
> Please hold for your number.

Suddenly, the fridge shudders. Sara jumps.

CUT BACK TO:

INT. MARION'S APARTMENT

Finally Marion stands up:

>   MARION
> It's three already. We're making a big deal out of nothing.

>   TYRONE
>   (a bit too willing)
> Yeah, we can stop using. We proved it. Right now.

MARION

Harry, it's stupid to panic and think the world's coming to an end just 'cause we can't score any solid weight.

HARRY

OK, fine.

Flick, sizzle, snap, suck, slap, rush, sigh . . .

And:

Crinkle, sprinkle, flick, drift, suck, sigh . . .

And then again:

Flick, sizzle, snap, suck, slap, rush, sigh . . .

CUT TO:

INT. MARION'S APARTMENT – MIDDLE OF THE NIGHT

Harry and Marion twist and turn in their bed. The sheets are covered in sweat.

Finally, Marion bolts up in bed gasping for breath. Harry turns on the light.

HARRY

You alright?

MARION
(*nods*)
Must have had a bad dream, I guess.

CUT TO:

INT. MARION'S KITCHEN.

Harry fills a glass of water. He notices that the spot where he normally shoots up in his inner arm is sore and red.

CUT BACK TO:

INT. MARION'S APARTMENT

Marion is still panting when Harry returns with a glass of water.

                            MARION
      Maybe we should dip in now.

                            HARRY
      It's all we have.

                            MARION
      Tyrone will score in the morning.

                            HARRY
      It's a bitch out there.

                            MARION
      It'll be fine, sweetheart, I just know it will.

A long beat.

                            HARRY
      Yeah, I guess. I'll get the stuff.

                            MARION
      I love you, Harry.

Relief. For now. Crinkle, sprinkle, flick, drift, suck, sigh . . .

CUT TO:

INT. SARA'S APARTMENT

Pop, hit, gulp, snap.

Sara downs a cup of coffee and goes to the phone.

Out of the corner of her eye she watches the fridge. She dials a number.

                    COMPUTERIZED OPERATOR
                         (*off-screen*)
      Welcome to Malin & Block. If you know your party's
      extension, please enter it now. For the directory please press
      four, one, one.

Sara presses 411.

      Please enter the last name of the person you are trying to
      reach.

SARA

Russel. Lyle Russel.

Sara starts to press some numbers.

COMPUTERIZED OPERATOR
(*off-screen*)

We're sorry, there's no one in the directory with that name.
Please wait for an operator.

A moment later an operator answers.

WOMAN ON PHONE
(*off-screen*)

Malin & Block.

SARA

Lyle Russel.

WOMAN ON PHONE
(*off-screen*)

I'm sorry, but I don't have his name listed on my directory.

SARA

The television.

WOMAN ON PHONE
(*off-screen*)

What television?

SARA

I don't know. I want to find out.

WOMAN ON PHONE
(*off-screen*)

Hold on a second.

Then, a loud shudder! The fridge is vibrating. Sara doesn't know what to do.

ANOTHER WOMAN ON PHONE
(*off-screen*)

Can I help you?

SARA

I want to speak to Lyle Russel.

ANOTHER WOMAN ON PHONE
(*off-screen*)

Who's that?

SARA

He called me and said I was going to be on a show and –

ANOTHER WOMAN ON PHONE
(*off-screen*)

Just a minute. I'll connect you with the programs department.

Sara waits as the phone rings and rings and the fridge continues to vibrate unnaturally.

THIRD WOMAN ON PHONE
(*off-screen*)

Can I help you?

SARA

I want Lyle Russel.

THIRD WOMAN ON PHONE
(*off-screen*)

Lyle Russel? Are you sure you have the right number?

SARA

He's putting me on a show.

THIRD WOMAN ON PHONE
(*off-screen*)

A show? What show?

Still on the phone, Sara slowly walks over to the fridge.

I'm afraid I don't understand. If you can't tell me –

SARA

He called me and said I'm going to be on TV and he sent me papers. I sent them back a long time already and I still don't know when –

THIRD WOMAN ON PHONE
(*off screen*)

Oh, I understand. Just a moment.

Some more clicks. Sara can barely stand. As she gets to the fridge, it slowly stops vibrating. Sweat is building.

FOURTH WOMAN ON PHONE
(*off-screen*)

Can I help you?

Carefully, Sara examines the fridge. She's having a hard time talking.

Hello?

SARA

Lyle Russel.

FOURTH WOMAN ON PHONE
(*off-screen*)

Who?

SARA

Lyle Russel?

FOURTH WOMAN ON PHONE
(*off-screen*)

Are you sure you have the right department?

And then, suddenly, the entire fridge quakes violently! Sara drops the phone and runs to her bedroom. On the phone:

Hello? Hello?

CUT TO:

INT. MARION'S APARTMENT – LATE MORNING

Marion expectantly watches Harry on the phone. Harry hangs up.

MARION

Well?

HARRY

Tyrone hasn't found anything.

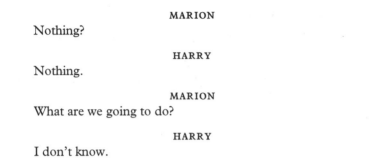

MARION

Nothing?

HARRY

Nothing.

MARION

What are we going to do?

HARRY

I don't know.

MARION

Well, you have to do something. It's your fault we don't have something for the morning.

HARRY

What are you talking about?

MARION

You were all hot in the biscuit to get off last night.

HARRY

That's all bullshit.

MARION

You didn't have to and we could have had something now.

HARRY

Whatta am I gonna do? Just sit and watch you push off and not go myself?

MARION

Then, just don't put all the weight on me, that's all. And leave me alone.

Pissed beat.

HARRY

I'm gonna go meet Ty.

CUT TO:

INT. TYRONE'S CLOSET

Harry and Tyrone open the shoe box. They grab the last cash in it.

> HARRY
> Don't worry. We'll fill it up again, man. Things'll get better soon, then we'll be puttin' the bread back in the box.

CUT TO:

EXT. CITY STREETS – NIGHT

Harry and Tyrone wait by a payphone on an abandoned street corner.

> HARRY
> I gotta call my mom. I just don't know what to do with her.

> TYRONE
> Ahm glad ah doan't have no one laying that kind of heavy motha shit on me, Jim. You honkies are too much with that guilt shit.

> HARRY
> Krist, you ain't kiddin', man. I sometimes think we'd be better without moms.

> TYRONE
> Ah doan' know, man. Mah mom died when ah was eight, but I remember she was one groovy woman. She have seven kids, Jim, an she was all big like an' all the time singin' and smilin'. She have a big chest like this and she used to cuddle me, Jim, an' ah remember how good it felt in there an' how sweet she smell. You know, she sing an' it make you feel good all ovuh, jus' like dope.

Small laugh in the freezing cold. Then, a Snot-faced Dealer rounds the corner and nods to Tyrone.

INT. SARA'S APARTMENT

The phone rings! Sara sticks her head out of the bedroom.

She looks at the fridge. It's quiet and still. She sneaks to the lazy chair and flips on the TV.

Then she answers the phone.

                              HARRY
                          (*off-screen*)
Hey, Ma. How ya doing?

                              SARA
                           (*scared*)
Oh, Harry.

                              HARRY
                          (*off-screen*)
I wanted to say hello, and that I'll visit soon.

Suddenly, the fridge hops, making a smashing noise. Sara sinks into her chair. Sara lets out a small scream.

Ma? You –

                              SARA
Can you come now? For a little while?

                              HARRY
                          (*off-screen*)
Ma, I'm tied up. I got a lot of irons in the fire and I have ta be around to take care of 'em.

The fridge hops again.

                              SARA
                          (*at fridge*)
Stop it!
                          (*to Harry*)
Not even a little visit? Please, Harry. Come over.

                              HARRY
                          (*off-screen*)
Hey, Ma, will you lighten up and stop playin' those guilt games with my head?

The fridge shakes and quivers like it's laughing.

                              SARA

   Please, Harry . . .

CUT TO:

EXT. CITY STREETS – SAME

Harry takes a deep breath into the phone. Tyrone rounds the corner,
smiling.

                              HARRY
                          (*into phone*)
   Look, Ma, I don't want to hassle you, okay? I loveya and I'll
see you soon. Take care.

                              SARA
                          (*off-screen*)
   Harry, it's all confusing and –

Harry hangs up and the two of them rush off.

CUT TO:

EXT. UNDER THE BOARDWALK – NIGHT

Flick, sizzle, snap, suck, slap, rush, sigh . . .

                             TYRONE
   So you want to hear the news?

                             HARRY
   What news?

                             TYRONE
   The good news and the bad news.

                             HARRY
   Shoot.

                             TYRONE
   The good news is that in a couple of days they'll be prime on
the streets.

                               77

HARRY
(*psyched*)

Really!

(*suspicious*)

Who told you?

TYRONE

Angel says Sal the Geep has sent word to let go a couple a keys for the Christmas season, he being a good Christian an' not wantin' anybody to be wantin' during this glorious season.

HARRY

You believe it?

TYRONE

I didn't until I heard the bad news.

HARRY

Yeah . . .

TYRONE

The price is doubled and you have to cop for weight, at least half a piece.

HARRY

How much?

TYRONE

Two.

HARRY

Fuckin' insane!

TYRONE

What you gonna do? The man ain't goin' to lay no nickel bag on you, thas foe damn sure.

HARRY

Where we gonna get two?

CUT TO:

INT. MARION'S APARTMENT

Marion can't believe what Harry just suggested.

MARION

You mean Arnold?

HARRY

Well your parents won't even take your call.

MARION

I haven't seen him in months.

HARRY

So what? He's still callin', ain't he?

MARION

Yes, but I don't know.

Marion stares into Harry's eyes – pleading.

HARRY

Look, I don't know what else to do. This is our last chance to get back on track. We won't have ta scuffle and make that freezing scene every day. We need the bread.

MARION

Getting the bread is not the problem, Harry –

HARRY

Then what's the problem, fa krist's sake?

MARION

I just don't know what I'll have to do to get it.

Harry gets it. Marion gets it. But for Harry, this is too important. He gets down and holds her hand:

HARRY

Look baby, this is our last chance to get back on track. We'll be back in bizness in no time. We'll start moving again and we'll start saving again. It'll happen, Marion.

Marion looks into him. Then, she gives him a gentle nod.

CUT TO:

INT. DOCTOR PILL'S EXAMINING ROOM

Doctor Pill smiles while Sara looks around wild-eyed.

DOCTOR PILL

What seems to be the problem? The weight is doing fine.

SARA

The weight is fine. I'm not so good. The refrigerator –

Suddenly, she looks around terrified.

DOCTOR PILL

Something wrong?

SARA

Things are all mixed up. Confused like –

DOCTOR PILL

Well, that's nothing to worry about.

He scribbles out a prescription.

Just give this to the nurse and make an appointment for a week.

Now, Sara is alone staring at the paper. TIGHT ON *paper. It reads* 'VALIUM'.

CUT TO:

INT. RAOUL'S CAFE – NIGHT

A dimly lit café. Marion wears lots of make-up and a long-sleeve blouse.
Arnold is worried.

> MARION
> No, no, I've just had the flu forever it seems like.

> ARNOLD THE SHRINK
> Are you depressed?

> MARION
> No, it's nothing like that. Just been very busy. I've been
> designing nonstop.

> ARNOLD THE SHRINK
> That's wonderful, I'm glad to hear you've been productive.

He smiles and touches her hand.

> To be perfectly straight, I was surprised to hear from you. Is
> something wrong?

MARION

No, why?

ARNOLD THE SHRINK

That's usually the case when someone calls whom you haven't heard from for a while.

MARION

No, everything's fine, but I do have a favor to ask.

He smiles and leans back into his chair. His smugness bothers her so she grabs her fork and stabs it into the back of his hand. Blood spurts out and she screams:

YOU SMUG SONOFABITCH!

A moment later, everything is back to normal. Marion was fantasizing.

ARNOLD THE SHRINK
(*grin*)

A favor? What is it?

MARION

I need to borrow some money.

CUT TO:

INT. ARNOLD THE SHRINK'S MANHATTAN CRASH PAD

In the bedroom, Marion slowly takes off her clothes. She's dying and almost crying.

Arnold, big smile, big erection (for him), watches her.

ARNOLD THE SHRINK

May I ask why?

MARION

Could you turn off the light?

ARNOLD THE SHRINK

Why do you want the light off?

MARION

I just do.

ARNOLD THE SHRINK

You never did before.

MARION

Please, Arnold.

Shrugging, he remote controls off the light. Arnold creeps up behind her and starts planting kisses on her.

Very gently, she begins to cry.

CUT TO:

INT. MARION'S APARTMENT

Harry scratches some vinyl. He takes the LP and frisbees it into the wall. It shatters!

Then, he collapses onto Marion's couch, picks up the remote and flips on the set. He tries to watch but he keeps looking at the clock.

Then, he hears the sounds of sex. He looks up on the TV and sees Marion fucking some dude with a hairy back. So, Harry lies on the ground and reaches for something under the couch.

Then: flick, sizzle, snap, suck, rush, sigh . . .

The image on the set slowly starts to dissolve back to the normal TV show.

Harry, a bit more comfortable, reclines on the couch and nods.

CUT TO:

INT. ARNOLD THE SHRINK'S MANHATTAN CRASH PAD – HALLWAY

At the front door Arnold, wrapped in a sheet, hands Marion some money. She leaves and he quickly locks the door.

Down the hallway and into –

THE ELEVATOR

– as anger, disgust and who knows what else billow up inside her. Her eyes begin to tear. Then –

83

ON THE STREET

– she leans against the building and vomits.

CUT TO:

INT. MARION'S APARTMENT

Marion crawls out of her winter clothes and joins Harry on the couch.

They sit on either side of the couch not looking at each other.

CUT TO:

INT. TYRONE'S NEW PAD

Tyrone, in his bikini underwear, stares at a picture of his mom.

Alice is gone.

He looks at the window. It's night-time and it's sleeting.

> TYRONE
Sheeit.

Tyrone starts to get dressed.

CUT TO:

INT. SARA'S BEDROOM – NIGHT

Pop, gulp, hit, snap . . .

Sara puts on some make-up. Her hand is not steady and her work is far from perfect. The lipstick is lopsided. The mascara is caked on one set of eyelashes.

In the red dress, with very little energy, she spins in front of the mirror.

She starts a dumpy version of a waltz. Very slowly. Her eyes are sunken and dark-ringed. Flesh hangs from her upper arms and neck.

CUT TO:

INT. MODERN SUPERMARKET – NIGHT

Harry and Tyrone stroll the aisles with an empty shopping cart. They eye other customers, most of whom are junkies trying to act nonchalant and making believe they're shopping. In actuality they're just trying to figure out what the fuck's going on.

                    TYRONE
    You dig the action, man.

                    HARRY
    Yeah, I feel like I'm dreamin'.

                    TYRONE
    I watch your back, you watch mine.

                    HARRY
    What are we supposed to do?

                    TYRONE
    I don't know. All they said was be at Waldbaum's.

Just then, they round a corner and spot a Pony-tailed Junkies walking into the back loading area. They follow.

CUT TO:

INT. MARION'S APARTMENT

Marion impatiently circles the apartment. She's very anxious.

CUT TO:

INT. SUPERMARKET LOADING AREA – LATER

Harry and Tyrone join a mass of smoking junkies in the back of the supermarket. Everyone is crowded in by the towering boxes of produce and canned goods.

HARRY
Everyone and their mother.

A moment later, the steel roll-gate starts to open. All the junkies turn to look.

Then, an eighteen-wheeler starts backing into the loading dock. 'IRVING'S FLORIDA ORANGES' is painted onto the truck.

When the truck stops at the dock, two White Heavies emerge from the front cab. They wear ski masks and carry glistening machine guns.

Sitting behind a table in front of the crates of oranges is a distinguished Bald Man sporting a white fur coat. He is flanked by two other heavies with masks and machine guns.

The junkies applaud! The two men unlock the back of the truck.

The Bald Man pops open two steel suitcases on the table. Harry, Tyrone and all the junkies push forward. The men with guns try to control them.

CUT TO:

INT. MARION'S APARTMENT

Marion, still circling, starts searching the apartment. She rips open her bureau, flips through clothes and unknowingly tosses her clothing sketches.

They slowly drift to the floor.

CUT TO:

EXT. SUPERMARKET LOADING AREA – LATER

Harry and Tyrone push their way to the front. A few lucky junkies hand the Bald Man money and get their dope. The heavies scream at the junkies to calm down or they're outta here.

Then suddenly, Harry spots a Gap-toothed Junkies pulling a gun. The men with the machine guns see him and pull out their guns. Harry grabs Tyrone and starts to pull him away when suddenly:

Bang!

Gap-tooth's gun goes off. It hits some oranges behind the Bald Man. The heavies let loose. Bullets everywhere!

Harry and Tyrone head for the supermarket in front. Boxes are blowing up around them.

The Bald Man slams the steel suitcases closed and starts pulling the truck doors closed.

Harry and Tyrone charge into the –

INT. SUPERMARKET – SAME

– with a bunch of other junkies. They rush down an aisle when the Pony-tailed Junkie gets nailed in front of them. He slides across the linoleum leaving a trail of blood behind him.

Harry and Tyrone leap over the dead body and rush –

OUTSIDE

– just in time to spot the eighteen-wheeler whiz by. Some of the junkies give chase. Harry thinks about it but Ty stops him. Instead, they quickly duck out.

CUT TO:

INT. TYRONE'S OLD DIVE PAD

Tyrone puffs on a cigarette while Harry paces.

> HARRY
>
> Stupid fucking junkie. Fucked. We are fucked. That's the last shit for miles.

> TYRONE
>
> Muthafuckas going back to Florida, sitting on their asses in sun while we're up here ass-deep in snow.

> HARRY
>
> Damn it. What are we gonna do now?
> > *(then an idea)*
> Hey. What would happen if we went down there to cop?

> TYRONE
>
> Now you're talking – sunny F.L.

> HARRY
>
> Yeah. Everybody's up here scufflin' to stay alive and gettin' ripped off or knocked off, and nobody's thought about goin' right to the fuckin' source.

> TYRONE
>
> You're serious?

> HARRY
>
> Why not?

> TYRONE
>
> What the fuck you talkin' about? Goin' up to the muthafuckin' room clerk at some hotel an' askin' for a connection?

> HARRY
>
> C'mon, Ty, get with it, eh? You tellin' me you can't nose out some dope when it's around?

> TYRONE
>
> You are serious. Tha's here, man. The Apple's mah neighborhood. What the fuck ah know about Miami? Them muthafuckin' Italians ain't sittin' aroun' jus' waitin' for me to show up, Jim.

HARRY

Dope smells the same there as it does here.

TYRONE

Yeah, but it's a long-ass walk, man.

HARRY

Not if you're drivin'. Look man, it's colder than hell and
those streets are hotter'n a bitch. After tonight . . . shit. Guys
are gettin' knocked off like they're givin' away season tickets
for every dead fiend.

TYRONE

That's no lie, Jim.

HARRY

Man, we got nothin' to lose, and we got to do it now while we
still have a few bucks.

TYRONE

If it's such a good idea why ain't somebody else thought of it?

HARRY

Because they're assholes. And that's just it. Nobody else has
thought of it. It's wide open and if we get there before anyone
else we can name our own price and sit back an' be cool and
have those fools scufflin' the streets for us.

TYRONE

Las' summer was a ball, Jim . . . Seems like a thousan' years
since las' summer. Sheeit.

HARRY

It'll be back like that, but only better. This is the kinda set up
you dream about.

TYRONE
(*starts to give in*)

You know, Angel can probably get us a short if we promise
him some dynamite scag.

HARRY

You think?

TYRONE
(*gives in*)
That muthafucka can dig up anything, even the daid.

CUT TO:

INT. SARA'S APARTMENT

Sara peeks her head into the living room, all the shades and curtains are drawn. She quietly tiptoes to the window and peeks out through the side of the shade.

Then she tiptoes over to the front door. Very carefully, she removes the tape over the peephole. The hallway is empty. She retapes the peephole.

Suddenly, the fridge lurches at her. It slides a good foot towards her. She jumps and runs to her viewing chair.

CUT TO:

INT. MARION'S APARTMENT

Marion rips through the apartment as she searches for something, anything.

She sinks to the floor and starts to sob. Just then, Harry walks in on her on the floor.

MARION
(*gets up, screams*)
Where have you been? I've been waiting all night.

HARRY
Where the hell do you think I've been?

MARION
Where's the score?

HARRY
Some dumb-ass junkie –

MARION
Did what? You fucked it up! Don't tell me you fucked it up!

HARRY

I didn't fuck it up. Me and Ty have a plan.

MARION

A plan!? I don't want another plan, I want my stuff!

HARRY

What the fuck's wrong with you?

MARION

Me!? You promised that everything was gonna be OK. I fucked that sleazebag – I put myself through hell for you. So what the fuck do you have for me?!

HARRY

What do you want from me? I don't have anything, nothing, there's nothing out there.

MARION

I don't give a shit. You loser. You fucking loser, I want you to come through for me.

HARRY

Ya think I'm playin' fuckin' games, for krist's sake? You wanna have some extra stuff?

Harry calls Tyrone. He grabs the picture of him and Marion in front of the store.

We were hipped to a dude that's holding some weight, but he ain't sellin'.

TYRONE
(*off-screen*)

Yeah.

HARRY

Give me that guy's number. The guy who likes broads.

TYRONE
(*off-screen*)

Big Tim? What for?

HARRY

Just give me the number, for krist's sake.

91

TYRONE
(*off-screen*)
OK, OK. Nine three four . . .

HARRY
You worried so goddam much . . .

Harry hangs up on Ty and hands Marion the number on the back of the photo.

Here, go fix yourself up with'im. You won't have to wait so long, and I won't have ta freeze my ass off in the fuckin' streets.

MARION
Fuck you.

HARRY
No, fuck you!

Harry charges out of the apartment. Marion stares after him. We float out of focus.

CUT TO:

INT. SARA'S APARTMENT

Pop, hit, gulp, snap. The fridge lurches another foot towards her.

She grabs the giant remote and flips on the TV. On the set is Tappy Tibbons:

TAPPY TIBBONS
Now let's meet our next winner. She's a beautiful woman with a winning sense of humor and a magical smile. She's really gonna win your heart. Straight from Brighton Beach, Brooklyn, let's give a juicy welcome to our very own Mrs Sara Goldfarb.

Red Sara marches out to applause.

TAPPY AND AUDIENCE
Juice by Sara! Juice by Sara! Juice by Sara! ooooOOOOH! Sara's got juice! Sara's got juice! ooooOOOOH Sara!

RED SARA

Thank you. Thank you. Oh Mr Tibbons, it's –

TAPPY TIBBONS

Tappy, please.

The fridge lurches again! She tries to ignore it and watch TV:

RED SARA

OK, Tappy. It's a pleasure to be here.

TAPPY TIBBONS

Well, it's a pleasure to have you. And that is one gorgeous outfit you have.

RED SARA

Oh thank you, Tappy. I just want to say hello to my husband, Seymour, and my beautiful successful son, Harold. Hello, Harold. I hope you're happy. I hope you're in love. Please come and see me and bring Marion, won't you?

The fridge slides closer. She fights not to look.

TAPPY TIBBONS

Hah hah. I'm sure he'll be here soon. It's time to start now, are you ready?

RED SARA

Oh yes. I'm ready, I'm ready.

TAPPY TIBBONS

After you . . .

Tappy motions towards the camera as the audience begins to applaud.

And then, Red Sara disappears. Sara hears something.

She looks to her right and sees Red Sara standing in her living room. Sara is shocked.

SARA

What are you doing?

Red Sara doesn't answer, she just huffs and humphs as she inspects the apartment.

Who are you? What do you want?

Red Sara continues to ignore her as she looks down her nose at the apartment. Then Red Sara waves at Tappy Tibbons.

RED SARA

Tappy!

TAPPY TIBBONS

Oh, I thought you'd never ask. Excuse me, everybody.

Tappy disappears from the screen. And now he too is with Red Sara in Sara's living room.

Sara sits in her chair, dumbfounded. She starts to get more and more upset as Tappy and Red Sara laugh at her furnishings and chatchkas.

SARA

What do you expect? I'm all alone. Could you do better? It's an old building. Ten years no painting, maybe more.

Red Sara and Tappy walk behind Sara's chair towards the windows.

I'm old. Alone. You don't understand. I'm trying. I'm trying. Please, please, I'll explain.

Now, Tappy and Red Sara laugh as they point at the TV. Sara looks over. On the TV she sees herself in her viewing chair. A giant, fanatic audience surrounds her – laughing and pointing.

Then there's a giant C-R-A-C-K!!! as Sara's walls split apart. Suddenly, she's on a television set. Two TV cameras slide in on her.

A Make-up Artist and Sound Man bum rush her. The man tries to put a mic on her while the woman tries to touch up her face.

No! No! Please, leave me alone!

The studio audience is going bananas laughing at her.

Cameras and TV cables stretch across the floor. Then the First Assistant Director by camera one cues her:

FIRST ASSISTANT DIRECTOR

Ready, Mrs Goldfarb, three, two, one . . .

He points at Sara and a bright spotlight falls on her.

Suddenly, Tappy and Red Sara lead a cha-cha line around Sara's lazy chair. Various weirdos, freaks and girls in bikinis join in.

Sara is terrified.

The fridge leaps towards her. Sara cries onto her wrinkled red dress.

She sinks to the floor. She crawls to the TV and begs:

> SARA
> Oh please . . . please . . . let me on the show . . . please . . . please . . . any show . . . please . . .

The partying gets louder and louder. Red Sara is French kissing Tappy Tibbons in Sara's lazy chair.

The fridge is only a few feet from her.

> RED SARA
> Feed me, Sara. Feed me.

Tappy joins in:

TAPPY TIBBONS

Feed me. Feed me.

Now the other freaks in the room and the studio crew:

FREAKS AND CREW

Feed me. Feed me. Feed me.

And now, the audience on the TV is chanting it:

AUDIENCE

Feed me. FEED ME. FEED ME.

The fridge towers over her. Suddenly, metal is tearing and the fridge has a mouth. Freon sprays out of its opening. The giant metal mouth lurches at Sara threatening to bite her.

Sara screams and bolts out of her home leaving the front door to her abandoned apartment wide open.

HARD CUT TO:

BLACK

ON THE SCREEN IN WHITE LETTERS: 'WINTER'

CUT TO:

EXT. BRIGHTON BEACH AVENUE – DAY

Sara manically marches down the street. The world shoots by her. A train roars by on the elevated tracks up above.

CUT TO:

INT. PONTIAC VENTURA CROSSING VERRAZANO'S BRIDGE – NIGHT

Harry and Tyrone ride in a beat-up 1972 Pontiac Ventura 2. Harry drives.

TIGHT ON *the car tuner. Tyrone spins the dial. Hip-hop blasts on the radio.*

Then Tyrone turns on the heat.

HARRY

Thank you, Angel.

TYRONE

Ah sure hope this mutha works. Ah could use some heat.

Ty sparks a joint.

How long will it take?

HARRY

We'll make it in a day, easy.

TYRONE

California, here we come.

HARRY

It's Florida.

TYRONE

I know, Jim. I just feel like breaking out into song.

Hands slap five. Harry cringes when Tyrone hits his hand.

CUT TO:

INT. D-TRAIN SUBWAY CAR – MOVING

Sara sits on the subway. Her hair sticks to her wet face. She turns to the strangers across from her.

SARA

I'm going on television. Today I'll find out when.

It's New York: of course she's ignored.

CUT TO:

INT. MARION'S APARTMENT

Marion sobs into the phone. She shreds the upholstery on the couch.

MARION

Florida!? Florida!? When's he gonna be back?

ANGEL
(*off-screen*)

I don't know. A few days.

MARION

Days!? What am I supposed, to do? You gotta help me!

ANGEL
(*off-screen*)

It's dry –

MARION

I can get you money, from my parents.

ANGEL
(*off-screen*)

Money means shit.

MARION

Please. Angel! Please!

ANGEL
(*off-screen*)

It's a drought. I ain't got nothing.

MARION

Please! Angel! Please!

CUT TO:

INT. MALIN & BLOCK – RECEPTION AREA

A Secretary looks up, startled. In front of her is Sara. Sara's hair and body are wet and she is wobbly.

The Secretary stares at Sara, not knowing what to do.

SARA

Why aren't you calling me? I have to know when I'm going to be on television. I'm Sara Goldfarb and you should tell me when I'm going to be on television.

SECRETARY

Just sit for a moment. I'll ring them.

Sara wobbles to a chair. She's confused and disorientated. Some office women come out from inside the office and huddle around her. Some security guards appear as well.

Sara tries to stand but she falls over and lands back in the chair.

The women tell her to stay seated.

>   SARA
> I need to know when maybe you lost my card, please, Dolly, you'll look and let –

>   OFFICE WOMAN
> Get her a cup of soup. Tell Mary to call an ambulance. Just relax, Mrs Goldfarb, everything will –

>   SARA
>   (*cries*)
> It's not the prizes. I'll give them away to the poor, I just want to be on the show. I'm waiting so long to be on with my Harry and grandson –

The Secretary returns with a mug filled with soup.

>   SECRETARY
> Here, Mrs Goldfarb, sip this.

>   OFFICE WOMAN
> Sometimes it takes awhile to get called for a show, Mrs Goldfarb.

CUT TO:

INT. PONTIAC VENTURA ON JERSEY TURNPIKE – DAWN

Tyrone drives. TIGHT ON *the tuner. The radio plays alternative rock.*

>   TYRONE
> Sheeit, the heater is just fine. I guess this ain't goin' to be such a bad trip.

>   HARRY
> Yeah, it's no big thing.

TYRONE
(*checks odometer*)

We's a couple a hundred miles closer to Miami, Jim. Let's stop at the next pit and take a taste.

HARRY

Yeah. Betta drop a few dexies too and get some coffee.

TYRONE

Right on.

CUT TO:

INT. MALIN & BLOCK – RECEPTION AREA

A crowd watches Sara babble. Two Paramedics arrive.

PARAMEDIC
(*to his partner*)

Looks like shock.

(*to Sara*)

Can you walk?

SARA

I'm walking across the stage and you should see my Harold on television. We're giving the prizes away. I just want to be on television.

PARAMEDIC
(*to women*)

Do you know her name?

OFFICE WOMAN #1

We think it's Sara Goldfarb.

SARA

The announcer is calling me Little Red Riding Hood, call Seymour and tell him to pick me up at the beauty parlor. I've got the red dress I wore at Harry's graduation and the gold shoes.

PARAMEDIC
(*gently*)

Okay, Mrs Goldfarb, let's just take it nice and easy. Here we go.

And the paramedics help poor Sara to her feet. They head to the elevator. Sympathy from the staring office women.

CUT TO:

INT. MARION'S APARTMENT

Marion stares at Big Tim's number. A moment later she picks up the phone and dials.

> BIG TIM
> (*off-screen*)

Yeah?

Marion hangs up. A long beat. Then she dials again.

Yeah!?

> MARION
> (*nervous*)

Hi . . .

Big Tim lets go a big laugh.

CUT TO:

INT. AMBULANCE – MOVING

Sara is strapped to a gurney. She mumbles to herself.

> SARA

Oh, Harry. I'm going to be on television.

CUT TO:

INT. PONTIAC VENTURA PARKED IN HO JO LOT

Flick, sizzle, snap, suck, slap, rush, sigh . . .

Tyrone leans against the driver's door – high.

Harry rolls up his sleeve. Right in the crotch of his arm is a nasty hole from shooting too much. It's infected and rings of red surround it.

> TYRONE

Sheeit. How long you got that?

A few days.

TYRONE

That don't look too good, Jim.

HARRY

It don't feel too good either. But a little stuff'll take care of that.

TYRONE

Don't shoot in there.

HARRY

I'll blow it if I don't. Fuck it.

Flick, sizzle, snap, suck, slap – break from the montage. For the first time we see a TIGHT CLOSE-UP *of a needle going into the hole, then we end the montage – rush, sigh . . .*

CUT TO:

INT. BELLEVUE HOSPITAL

Sara, on her gurney, is pushed through crowded corridors of a hospital. The noise and chaos reach her in surreal muffled tones.

She's mumbling to herself – dreaming of being on television. Then she's slid into the emergency room.

Young, serious Doctor Spencer shines a light into her eye. Sara tries to smile.

DOCTOR SPENCER

No emergency. Take her to psyche.

CUT TO:

EXT. APARTMENT BUILDING ENTRANCE

A security camera studies Marion as she waits at the front door. Buzz! Marion pushes the door open and enters.

CUT TO:

EXT. BIG TIM'S APARTMENT

Big Tim's door opens wide, revealing an even wider Big Tim.

Big Tim is big in every way. His body is big, his smile is big, his laugh is big and even his apartment is big.

> BIG TIM

Come in.

He steps aside and Marion enters the huge living room with a grand view of Prospect Park.

Big Tim takes her coat.

Have a seat. What would you like?

> MARION
> (*meek*)

Nothing.

> BIG TIM

Oh, you strictly a dope fien'?

Marion is startled by Big Tim's comment. She recovers.

> MARION

Oh, maybe I'll have a little chartreuse.

> BIG TIM

Yellow or green?

> MARION
> (*surprised*)

Oh, ahhh . . . yellow.

Big Tim joins her with the drinks. He takes out a hash pipe and sparks it. Marion is offered the pipe and she takes a few pokes.

> BIG TIM

What's your name?

> MARION

Marion.

Big Tim's laugh is loud, deep and happy – a presence of its own.

BIG TIM

What you know, Maid Marion. I'm Little John.

Big Tim pulls Marion into his chest. She lets him.

You know what I like best about patty chicks?

Marion smiles as she relaxes into him.

They give good head. Black broads don't know nothing about giving head. I don't know why. Might be it has something to do with some ancient tribal custom.

Big laugh from Big Tim. He pulls Marion up to him and kisses her. After a beat, she kisses back. Then, he backs off.

Better save some of that energy.

She lies down on his stomach. Gently he turns her head around as he pulls out his penis.

She stares at Big Tim's joint knowing what she's supposed to do but not being able to do it. Her insides tremble and knot.

I know it's purty, baby, but I didn't take it out for air.

He nudges her and she grabs it and starts kissing it. Suddenly, she stops. She's going to be sick. Big Tim laughs his big laugh and points to the bathroom.

That way.

CUT TO:

INT. BIG TIM'S BATHROOM

Marion finishes barfing. She washes her face and mouth in the sink. She looks up at herself. She's trembling.

She shuts her eyes and we cut to –

BLACK –

We hear Marion breathe deeply. She collects herself.

Into the BLACK *rushes streams of* RED.

When she opens her eyes we are back in –

THE BATHROOM

Marion fixes her hair and smiles at herself.

CUT TO:

INT. BIG TIM'S LIVING ROOM

Big Tim laughs as Marion emerges from the bathroom.

> MARION
> Sorry. Must have been the chartreuse.

> BIG TIM
> Welcome back.

Marion's smile turns into an eager grin. He chuckles as she gets on her knees.

> Yeahhhh, little bo-peep done foun' her sheep.

Big Tim laughs his big laugh as we –

CUT TO:

INT. PONTIAC VENTURA SOMEWHERE ON I–95 – HEADING SOUTH

Tyrone drives while Harry squirms. His arm hurts like hell. TIGHT ON *tuner. The radio plays country and western.*

> TYRONE
> I told you to stay away from that arm, man.

> HARRY
> I gotta call Marion.

Tyrone watches the odometer changes from 599 to 600.

> TYRONE
> Well, it'll be long-distance now. That's six hundred. We six hundred damn miles closer to Miami.

> HARRY
> Yeah. We're also six hundred miles away from New York.

Afraid now, Tyrone looks out the window. The landscape is foreign and strange – almost alien.

CUT TO:

INT. BIG TIM'S BATHROOM

After sex, Big Tim opens the door and leans up against the doorway. Naked, he watches Marion as she finishes getting dressed. Marion can't look at herself in the mirror or at Big Tim.

> BIG TIM
> You know, baby, I can fix it so you can pick up a real, nice taste. Though it's more like play, baby. Sunday night we're having a gathering, all good people –

> MARION
> (*smiles*)
> No, I couldn't. I'm busy. And I'm not really hooked.

Big Tim laughs his big laugh and tosses her some bags.

> BIG TIM
> Yeah, I know. But I'm tellin' ya', it's a real nice taste.

Marion quickly grabs the bags and starts putting them in her purse.

> What the fuck you doing?

> MARION
> (*startled*)
> Nothing, I'm . . .

> BIG TIM
> Damn!
> (*laughs*)
> Damn, I got me some kinda virgin. Now you gotta be kidding ol' Tim, you just got to be.

> MARION
> I don't kn –

> BIG TIM
> You mean you not going to count what's there but you just

going to be puttin' it in your pocketbook and just walk out in the street? Damn! You sure haven't been around long, baby.

MARION
(flushed)

I'm not exactly a naive school girl, I . . . I . . . I've been all through Europe an' . . . an'. . . and I'm just not –

BIG TIM

Sheeit, ain't nothing to be ashamed of, baby, we all gotta get down with it for the first time. I ain't bad rappinya. I just don't want to see you get ripped off. Sheeit, you earned that baby and you sure as hell don't want to donate it to some purse snatcher.

He laughs. Marion smiles.

Lookit, there be one place you can stash ol' doogie without you worrying about it be accidently getting in the wrong hands, you dig? Ain't no purse snatcher or mugger going to rip you off there, baby.

As Marion catches on she flushes and nods her head.

Big Tim laughs his big laugh as he wanders into the living room.

I'll see you Sunday, Maid Marion.

Then Marion lifts up her skirt and does the deed.

CUT TO:

INT. PSYCHE WARD

Sara is strapped to a hospital bed. She sobs to herself.

The grey ward is packed with twice as many beds as there should be. Patients wander around in straitjackets. Screams of agony and pain barely reach her ears.

Doctor Spencer addresses Sara and tries to calm her.

DOCTOR SPENCER

Mrs Goldfarb. Please try and answer me. When did you start taking the pills?

SARA

When? The summer . . . Oh, this summer. I got a special
place in the sun. Ada fixed my hair.

DOCTOR SPENCER

You started in the summer. Last summer? OK Mrs
Goldfarb, everything will be alright, we'll fix you up in no
time.

SARA
(*grins*)

You're a good boy, Harold.

And for a moment, Doctor Spencer is Harry – golden smile and all.

CUT TO:

INT. MARION'S BATHROOM

*We look down on Marion's back from above the tub. She is bent over,
her head beneath the water between her knees. She holds her breath for
an eternity . . .*

*Then, we look into her face as she screams. Air bubbles shoot to the
surface.*

CUT TO:

EXT. I–95 – MAYBE GEORGIA

CUT TO:

INT. PONTIAC VENTURA

Tyrone still drives.

There's a preacher screaming gospel on the radio.

Harry squirms as he grabs his arm. He's wincing in pain.

HARRY

Man, I can't cut it. I gotta do something about this arm.

TYRONE

Let's see what it looks like.

Harry winces as he very carefully rolls up his sleeve.

The area around the hole is white and raised. Even worse, the area around the white is slightly green. Also, a wide, dark red streak reaches down his arm towards his hand.

They both stare at it for a moment.

> HARRY

Oh man.

> TYRONE

Sheeit, that be the ugliest mothafucka I've ever seen.

> HARRY

I gotta call Marion.

> TYRONE

Let's find a hospital first.

CUT TO:

INT. PSYCHE WARD

A needle punctures Sara's arm. The Nurse wipes off the blood that spills out.

In a surreal moment, the world slows down. Real slow.

Sara's tongue sticks to the top of her mouth. She pries it off with a rattling smack in her brain. Her mouth is dry and small drops of foam form on the sides of her chapped lips.

CUT TO:

INT. SOUTHERN DOCTOR'S EXAMINATION ROOM

To try and disperse the pain, Harry marches around the examination room. The pain is excruciating.

A grey-haired Southern Doctor comes in.

> SOUTHERN DOCTOR

What's the problem?

HARRY

My arm, it's killing me.

The Doctor looks for a moment. Then, he grabs Harry's arm and looks at it. Harry winces in pain.

SOUTHERN DOCTOR

I'll be back in a minute.

The Doctor leaves.

CUT TO:

INT. MARION'S APARTMENT

Marion stares at an empty pile of bags in front of her. Then she stares at the photo of her and Harry in front of the store. Next, she flips it over and looks at Big Tim's number. A moment later she picks it up and dials Big Tim.

BIG TIM
(*off-screen*)

Yeah!?

MARION
(*nervous*)

Hi . . .

Big Tim lets go a big laugh.

CUT TO:

INT. PSYCHE WARD

Two Male Attendants enter with a tray of food. They joke with each other and barely notice Sara.

They try to lift Sara up but she can't support herself.

Then they try harder and they shove her into a sitting position. One of the attendants puts some food in her mouth. She tries to swallow, but her throat isn't working.

ATTENDANT
(*slow motion*)
S-w-a-l-l-o-w! S–w–a–l–l–o–w!

But the food just dribbles out the side. As they continue their conversation about the Jets, they grab her and force the food down her throat by holding her nose and keeping her mouth shut.

Her eyes blast open in terror. Her head beats thunderously in her ears.

CUT TO:

INT. MARION'S APARTMENT

Marion puts mascara on her left eye. Then she puts on some clothes.

CUT TO:

INT. SOUTHERN DOCTOR'S WAITING ROOM

Tyrone flips through an old copy of Fortune Magazine. *He tries to ignore all the white folks gawking at him.*

Then he spots a pair of boots standing in front of him. Next, he spots the gun and baton.

Tyrone looks up into a towering Highway Cop's stern glare.

Cuff one wrist, cuff the other.

CUT TO:

INT. MARION'S APARTMENT

TIGHT ON *Marion's right eye as she carefully applies mascara. She puts on some more clothes.*

CUT TO:

INT. PSYCHE WARD

Doctor Spencer towers over Sara. He reads her chart and is concerned.

DOCTOR SPENCER
You have to eat, Mrs Goldfarb. If we're going to get you healthy again, you have to eat. Try to work with the

attendants. I'm going to try some new medications. They should help us.

He pats her on the shoulder and walks away. Sara tries to call for him, to make any noise, to plead, to do anything. But she can't.

A moment later, the two Male Attendants come for her. They grab her and move her into a wheelchair. Restraints for her arms and legs are slapped on.

They grab a clear plastic tube. They cover it with lubricant. Then they try to slide it into her nose.

Sara struggles until one attendant grabs her head and whacks it flat against a head rest.

ATTENDANT

OK, Miss, just relax. We're gonna try to help you to eat.

Pinned, they slide the tube into Sara's nose, down her throat and into her stomach.

Then the feeding begins.

CUT TO:

INT. MARION'S APARTMENT

TIGHT ON *Marion's lips as she puts on lipstick. Marion smacks her lips together.*

Marion in front of the full-length mirror is dressed to the hilt. She makes last minute corrections to her outfit when the phone rings.

Nervous, she answers.

MARION

Hello?

CUT TO:

INT. SOUTHERN JAIL PAYPHONE AREA — MARION'S APARTMENT

INTERCUT:

Harry in pain on the telephone. Marion sits by the phone.

HARRY

Marion.

MARION

Harry? Oh, Harry.

HARRY

Oh, Marion, I've been thinking about you. You're OK?

MARION

When you coming back?

HARRY

Soon. You're holding out right?

MARION

When?

HARRY

Soon. Everything's going to be alright.

MARION

Will you come today?

HARRY

Yeah, soon. Just wait for me. I'll be back soon. You'll wait,
right?

Marion doesn't answer. She closes her eyes.

Marion.

MARION

Yeah.

HARRY

Just wait.

MARION

I will, Harry.

HARRY

I'm coming, Marion. I am. And I'm sorry. I'm real sorry.

MARION

I know, Harry. I know.

A long beat. Silence. Slowly Marion hangs up.

BY THE PAYPHONES

– Harry hangs up. His sobs turn into his pain. His pain turns into his misery.

IN MARION'S APARTMENT

– Marion hangs up and wipes away her tears. She catches her image in the mirror and quickly finishes her mascara. Then: Crinkle, sprinkle, flick, drift, suck, sigh . . .

CUT TO:

INT. PSYCHE WARD – HALLWAY

Sara is still strapped to the wheelchair. Doctor Spencer smiles at her.

DOCTOR SPENCER
Mrs Goldfarb, are you alright?

Sara can't respond. She can only look. Doctor Spencer tries to be positive.

Mrs Goldfarb, we've tried several medications and you don't seem to be responding. I believe we've come to a point where we need to try some alternative methods. We've had excellent results with these techniques in the past. So if I can just get your John Hancock, we'll get underway.

Doctor Spencer hands Sara a pen. Somehow, she is able to sign.

CUT TO:

INT. HOLDING TANK

Harry is withdrawing in pain on his bunk. Tyrone is at the bars, sweating and dying.

HARRY
Jesus krist. I need a doctor.

> TYRONE
> (*through bars*)

My friend needs a doctor. Please. He needs a doctor.

> HARRY

I won't make it.

> TYRONE
> (*to Harry*)

Just hang tough, baby. Just hang tough.

> HARRY

Please! Please, Ma! Help me.

> TYRONE
> (*through bars*)

Help! Please!

> HARRY

Please, Maaaaaa!

CUT TO:

INT. PSYCHE WARD — HALLWAY

Sara is quickly unstrapped from her wheelchair. She's lifted up and placed onto a gurney. Her head hangs, lifeless. Then she's strapped down.

CUT TO:

INT. BIG TIM'S LUSH PAD

TIGHT ON *Marion's hand knocking on Big Tim's front door.* TIGHT ON *Big Tim's famous smile:*

> BIG TIM

Maid Marion. Welcome.

CUT TO:

INT. PSYCHE WARD — HALLWAY

Sara is wheeled quickly through the halls of the asylum.

CUT TO:

EXT. HOLDING TANK

Tyrone tries to keep Harry in line with all the convicts but Harry can barely stand.

A Court Doctor, followed by two Guards, moves from prisoner to prisoner.

Bored to death he looks into each prisoner's eyes with a mini-mag and says:

> COURT DOCTOR
> Can you hear me? Can you see me?

Each prisoner responds:

> PRISONER
> Yes, sir.

The doctor checks a box on a piece of paper.

> COURT DOCTOR
> OK for work.

The Guards chuckle.

CUT TO:

INT. PSYCHE WARD — HALLWAY

Sara continues her trip on the gurney. Terror enters her heart.

CUT TO:

EXT. HOLDING TANK

Now it's Tyrone's turn.

> COURT DOCTOR
> Can you hear me? Can you see me?

Tyrone nods. That isn't good enough, and so a guard whacks him in the back of the head.

> GUARD
> Say 'sir', nigga. God damn New Yawk dope fien' niggas. Learn some manners.

COURT DOCTOR

Can you hear me? Can you see me?

TYRONE

Yes, sir.

GUARD

Good boy.

They chuckle. The doctor moves down to Harry.

Harry can barely stand. His eyes are glazed over.

COURT DOCTOR

Can you hear me? Can you see me?

GUARD

Says he's got something wrong with his arm.

The doctor yanks Harry's sleeve up. Lightning pain:

HARRY
(*scream*)

Ma . . .

Harry collapses. The guards laugh at him as they pick him up.

GUARD

Your mommy isn't here.

The doctor looks at Harry's arm. The guards grab their noses and almost yack from the smell.

COURT DOCTOR

I don't think you'll be putting any more dope in that arm.

GUARD

Damn, it smells worse than he do.

COURT DOCTOR

Better get him over to the hospital. I don't expect he'll live out the week.

CUT TO:

INT. PSYCHE WARD – SHOCK THERAPY ROOM

Sara is unstrapped from the gurney. Then she is lifted off the gurney and laid on a table. Next she is strapped to the table.

She tries to struggle but the hands are too many, too strong.

CUT TO:

INT. BIG TIM'S LUSH PAD

We hear twenty men cheer as we glimpse into the room. They're all wearing suits and holding flashlights.

TIGHT ON *Marion's shocked face.* TIGHT ON *Big Tim's knowing smile.* TIGHT ON *cigars in strangers' mouths.* TIGHT ON *male hands clapping.* TIGHT ON *empty faces of five other pretty women checking out Marion.*

> BIG TIM
> (*whispers to Marion*)
> They be six of you cuttin' up an entire piece.

Marion looks at him.

> An' it be real good.

Marion accepts it. Then . . .

TIGHT ON *Big Tim's famous smile:*

> Show time.

The men shine their lights on Marion's clothed tits, her privates.

CUT TO:

INT. PSYCHE WARD – SHOCK THERAPY ROOM

Someone sticks something between Sara's teeth. The people around her talk casually and laugh occasionally.

She tries to look around but her body is immobile.

She can make out shadows on the edges of her vision but mostly all she sees are the lights above her.

Then she feels two cold metal discs placed against her temples.

CUT TO:

INT. EMERGENCY OPERATING ROOM

Harry is thrown onto an operating table. His clothes are gone in a blink of the eye.

A serious and focused Emergency Doctor steps in.

> EMERGENCY DOCTOR
> We're taking it off at the shoulder. Let's move here people, otherwise we lose him.

Harry remains semiconscious as the Anesthesiologist sticks a mask over his face.

Everything starts to go white. The Emergency Doctor starts up a circular saw.

Before everything is gone, Harry witnesses the doctor cutting into his shoulder.

CUT TO:

INT. PSYCHE WARD

Sara's heart pounds in her ears. She tries to scream, but a Technician interrupts her:

> TECHNICIAN
> (*off-screen*)
> OK, ready and one.

SMASH CUT TO:

BLINDING PRIMARY RED

We hear a crowd cheer!

CUT TO:

INT. BIG TIM'S LUSH PAD

In slow motion and tight close-ups we experience the orgy with Marion.

There's nipples, tongues, sex toys, eyes closed in ecstasy, men's glares, men's smiles and the like. The images aren't sexy, they're scary.

One of the girls holds up a double-headed dildo and says:

                              GIRL
   What should we do now?

A Pervert screams out:

                            PERVERT
   Ass to ass, ass to ass!

Marion complies and the flashlights shine. Then the Pervert starts a chant:

   Cum! Cum!

The other men join in as the pace quickens.

                 PERVERT AND ALL THE MEN
                  (building in pace and volume)
         Cum! Cum! CUM! CUM! CUM!! CUM!!!

Marion is at first afraid. Then, she closes her eyes. Her lips start to quiver. Big Tim's smile gets wider and wider and wider.

And then Marion comes.

CUT TO:

INT. PSYCHE WARD – SHOCK THERAPY ROOM

Sara's arched and stiffened body looks as if fire has just shot through her body.

Her eyes are almost popping out of her head as her mind screams AAAAAAAAAAAAAAHHHHHHHHHHHHHHHHHH . . .

She settles for a moment on the table.

Her heart does not beat, her lungs do not breathe.

A moment later, the breath returns. Then the heartbeat slowly emerges. And then, the Technician:

TECHNICIAN

OK, ready and two.

SMASH CUT TO:

PRIMARY RED

A crowd cheers!

Then we fade to:

PRIMARY BLUE

Then we –

CUT BACK TO:

INT. PSYCHE WARD

Once again Sara tries to scream in pain. Flames seem to sear every cell of her body and her bones feel like they are being twisted and crushed.

Smoke simmers off of her hair and skin.

As her body settles, it happens one last time:

TECHNICIAN

OK, ready and three.

SMASH CUT TO:

PRIMARY BLUE

The crowd cheers once more.

DISSOLVE TO:

EXT. CONEY ISLAND PIER

The pier stretches off into the beautiful sea. A woman in a red dress walks a baby carriage.

Now we're on Harry, looking healthy and vibrant. He screams for Marion!

121

But she doesn't hear him and she keeps walking. He runs after them.

When he gets close, he suddenly stops. Marion turns around. He reaches to hug her. But, as he does we are in –

BLACK

Harry gets terrified. He starts to scream for Marion.

> HARRY

Marion? Marion?!

He steps backwards off the edge of a cliff and rushes headfirst into a concrete sidewalk as he screams:

MARION!

And we –

CUT TO:

INT. HOSPITAL ROOM

An Angelic Nurse looks down upon Harry. Tubes stick into every part of him. His eyes are half-open.

She wipes the sweat from his brow.

> HARRY

Marion.

> ANGELIC NURSE

It's alright. Don't worry. You're in a hospital and you're going to be just fine.

> HARRY

Marion. Marion.

> ANGELIC NURSE

Who's that? She'll be sent for. She'll come. She loves you and she'll come.

Then Harry opens his eyes fully. For a moment he understands. He is an adult and he is calm.

> HARRY

No.

ANGELIC NURSE

No?

HARRY

No. She won't.

ANGELIC NURSE

She'll come.

HARRY

No. She won't.

And then Harry starts to cry. As we float up high above his bed we watch him curl up into a ball.

CUT TO:

EXT. JAIL MACHINE SHOP

Tyrone drills holes into metal plates with an oversized machine. He dry heaves and fights to stay in his seat. A Laughing Guard snickers at him.

CUT TO:

INT. MARION'S APARTMENT

At the foot of Marion's couch are the torn and smeared sketches of Marion's designs.

Marion comes in through the front door. She walks across the sketches and sits on the couch. She has lipstick smeared across her face.

She pulls out a large bag of dope and stares at it. Happily, she fondles the bag. Then, she hugs it tight against her bosom. Slowly, she curls up into a fetal position, content.

CUT TO:

INT. JAIL DORMITORY

The work gang collapse onto their individual bunks. Tyrone, sweaty and dirty, does the same.

He fights the cramps in his stomach for as long as he can until he passes out.

Then, Tyrone and his bed dissolve into the past. Young Tyrone rests in his mom's generous arms.

Finally, it is peaceful. Tyrone's mom brushes the tears from his eyes.

> TYRONE'S MOTHER
>
> How's your tummy feel?

> YOUNG TYRONE
>
> It's mostly gone, Momma. I doan' need no more medicine.

> TYRONE'S MOTHER
>
> That's my big boy.

He looks up at his mom as she starts to sing 'Hush little baby'.

> YOUNG TYRONE
>
> Your breath be all nice an' sweet, Mommy.

She hugs her son tight.

> TYRONE'S MOTHER
>
> The sweetness be in you, child, the sweetness be in you.

CUT TO:

INT. PSYCHE WARD – VISITING ROOM

Ada and Rae sit in the corner of the room stunned by their surroundings. Mounted on the wall is a television. Tappy Tibbons is on. No one is watching.

Sara shuffles towards them and they barely recognize her. Her grey roots match her grey skin which matches her grey gown.

Ada starts taking food out of a large shopping bag.

> ADA
>
> We got some lox and cream cheese and bagels and blintzes with sour cream and some danishes and pastrami and chopped liver on rye with mustard and onions and a container of tea and . . . How are you, Dolly?

But Sara doesn't answer. She can't. They put their hands on their friend's shoulders but nothing seems to reach her.

Then they notice that water is dripping down Sara's leg and onto the floor. Sara has urinated on herself.

CUT TO:

EXT. BUS STOP

Ada and Rae sit waiting for the bus on a grey day in front of a grey building. Tears flow from their eyes. They hug each other.

CUT TO:

INT. PSYCHE WARD

Sara lies on her bed. A tiny smile emerges on her face.

We get closer and closer to her until we go into the blackness of her pupil.

Deep in the blackness we see another world. It is a world of PRIMARY BLUE. *And sucking us into the blue is the roar of a crowd.*

And there with a giant smile is good ol' Tappy in black tie. He looks into the camera and says:

TAPPY TIBBONS
And our next winner is that delightful personality, straight from Brighton Beach, Brooklyn, please give a juicy welcome to Mrs Goldfarb.

Red Sara steps out and joins Tappy. She's overwhelmed.

TAPPY AND AUDIENCE
Juice by Sara! Juice by Sara! Juice by Sara! ooooOOOOH! Sara's got juice! Sara's got juice! ooooOOOOH Sara!

TAPPY TIBBONS
And Mrs Goldfarb, that's not it. I'm delighted to tell you that you've just won the grand prize.

RED SARA
Really?

TAPPY TIBBONS

Yes! How does it feel?!

RED SARA

It feels great. I feel wonderful. I feel amazing. This is great!

The audience goes crazy, they love it. And they start to chant:

AUDIENCE

We love Sara! We love Sara!

The chant continues . . .

TAPPY TIBBONS

They love you, Sara.

RED SARA

I love them. Oh, I love them.

TAPPY TIBBONS

Now let me show you what you've won. Your prize has a sweet smile and his own private business. He just got engaged and he's planning to get married this summer. Will you please give a juicy welcome to Mrs Sara Goldfarb's one and only son – Harry Goldfarb!

Harry walks out from back. The audience are out of their seats, screaming at the tops of their lungs. Sara is gushing!

TAPPY AND AUDIENCE

Juice by Harry! Juice by Harry! Juice by Harry!
ooooOOOOH! Harry's got juice! Harry's got juice!
ooooOOOOH Harry!

Harry walks out and hugs his mother.

RED SARA

Oh Harry, Harry, Harry. I love you, Harry.

HARRY

I love you too, Ma.

They hug and they hug as the audience scream their applause.

A smile fills Sara's beautiful face. Happiness. Total and complete love.

Except for the truth, the nagging reality. It means tears for Sara and her sparkling eyes well up with fantastic, warm tears.

But they don't damage her glorious smile.

FADE TO BLACK

CREDITS ROLL